ff

CARYL PHILLIPS

The Final Passage

narrative is
in English
— but speech in
vernac

— brmry

faber and faber

LONDON · BOSTON

First published in 1985
by Faber and Faber Limited
3 Queen Square London WC1N 3AU
Reprinted 1985, 1986 and 1987

Filmset by Wilmaset Birkenhead
Printed in Great Britain by
Redwood Burn Limited
Trowbridge, Wiltshire
All rights reserved

© Caryl Phillips, 1985

British Library Cataloguing in Publication Data

Phillips, Caryl
The final passage.
1. Title
823'.914[F] PR6066.H45/
ISBN 0-571-13438-6 Pbk

A people without history
Is not redeemed from time, for history is a pattern
Of timeless moments. So, while the light fails
On a winter's afternoon, in a secluded chapel
History is now and England.

T. S. ELIOT

For my Mother and Father

THE END

Leila pulled the baby boy even closer to her body. He was hungry and tired but she could not feed him here. Like the hundreds of others ageing patiently in the procession, he would have to wait. A uniformed young man (he looked scarcely more than an adolescent), sat imperiously at their head. He held the key to the gate through which they would soon pass. From there they would go down the slipway, into one of the small launches, then out to sea where they would transfer to the SS *Winston Churchill*. When exactly they would begin this first part of their journey Leila, like everyone else, was unsure. But, like the others, she felt it would be soon.

She and Calvin were near the front of the queue where they had been for nearly five hours. They had arrived around 6.30, anxious to secure a good place so they might get the cabin they had paid for. Rumour had it (and her mother had always told her there was a little truth in every rumour) that despite the markings on their tickets people just took whatever cabin they could find. If they could not find one they had to resign themselves to living on deck. Leila had paid for a cabin so she was making sure.

At 6.30 the harbour had been a blaze of colour and confusion. Bright yellows and brilliant reds, sweet smells and juices, a lazy deep sea nudging up against the land, and looking down upon it all the mountains ached under the weight of their dense green vegetation. Leila watched as the women sold their food, cursing, pushing, laughing. She listened as occasionally a tired voice still found the strength to soar.

'Come nuh, man, who want to buy peanut from me?'

9

As usual nobody did, and the woman fanned herself with a straw hat, her old, sun-blackened face gleaming with sweat. A small, angular boy stopped to tie up the frayed laces in his worn-out tennis shoes. Out of the corner of his eyes, he concentrated on the fresh peanuts scattered on her tray. Then her voice disturbed him.

'Well, boy, you want some or not?'

He smiled shyly, his white teeth a little too large, and a few too many, for his young mouth. The old woman pursed her lips and tossed her head.

'Boy, you want one?'

He pulled the fancy bows tight and stood up in such a way that the sun formed a halo around his head. He grinned at her, hesitated, then skipped away, his hacked-off oversized shorts brushing lightly against his thighs.

Then Leila watched as the fishing boats came home; and the fishermen quickly folded up their nets for the night before heading down-town to Jumbies rum bar. On the quayside somebody unhooked the 'Cruisers for charter' sign. (Every day around this time it looked as if it was ready to fall down of its own accord. Some day somebody would find another rusty nail and hang it up straight.) Then night approached and began to drain the sky of colour, and the sun laboured badly. And the battered suitcases and cardboard boxes began to appear, names scribbled on them in shaky white paint, their hopeful addresses pitched aimlessly at a point somewhere the other side of the world. In the gathering gloom the mosquitoes began to sing their high piercing tunes, and in the distance the bad dogs began to bark wildly with neither rhythm nor harmony. It became darker as night, undisturbed and confident, crept on.

'ALPHONSO EDWARDES, SLOUGH, NEAR BUCKS, ENGLAND, GREAT BRITAIN'.

'MRS H. O. S. SIMMONDS IN THE CARE OF L. J. SIMMONDS ESQ. OF SHEFFIELD, ENGLAND, YORKSHIRE'.

'PROPERTY OF LARRINGTON SEVILLE. TO BE HANDLED WITH CARE. DESTINED FOR LONDON COLLEGE OF LAW STUDIES. LONDON. ENGLAND. THANK YOU'.

Leila watched the darkness drop, and she listened as the noises of the day gave way to the noises of the night.

Michael had still not turned up. The young woman in front of Leila turned around and began to talk. Leila did not listen. She tried instead to imagine what Michael was thinking about. Last night, before he left for his grandmother's house, he had talked briefly. For the first time Leila had heard an almost candid apprehension in his voice.

'Leaving this place going make me feel old, you know, like leaving the safety of your family to go live with strangers.'

Leila stood by the table and watched the back of her husband's head. He sat in the doorway looking out across the rest of the village, and he spoke as if confessing to something.

'I met Footsie Walter's brother Alphonse in town last Saturday when I went in to carry the yams. He don't make it sound bad or nothing, but he make it sound a bit different from how I did imagine it.'

'Which is like what?'

'Better, I suppose.'

For a moment Leila had thought she must be mistaken. She wondered if Michael was consciously trying to create this mood or if he had really forgotten himself. Either way she went forward and put a hand on to his shoulder.

'I know things between us don't be so good at times,' he said, looking up at her, 'but it's like you're putting a chicken into a cardboard box. The thing bound to start jumping about a bit and loose off a few feathers.' He had laughed, then scraped back his chair and stood up. 'I'm beginning to sound like a preacher man.'

The young woman in front of Leila stopped talking. She pulled on a light blue cardigan over her sleeveless white dress. Leila had already anticipated the chill that would be coming in

11

off the sea and had wrapped her mother's bright orange shawl around her shoulders. She trapped Calvin in the warmth between her breasts. Her red skirt brushed freely against her skinny legs, and she curled her toes up in her sandals to try and keep her feet warm. The two of them, one with child, like matchstick figures in a large tapestry, stood together in silence. A little way offshore a flock of birds swooped and fell together as if held by invisible strings. They banked away out of sight.

Leila looked behind her and saw that the line meandered around the corner of the customs house. Some were standing, others sat on their boxes or suitcases, some sat on the concrete resting their backs against their luggage or each other. They were deep in thought and, at this late hour, spoke either in whispers or not at all. Relatives who had come to see off the voyagers were tired. The drink having been drunk, they had been told to go back home. Some had left, but those who stayed dozed off to sleep with unburdened minds. For Leila and everybody else minutes were hours and hours seemed like days and they were all waiting, still and alone, each silent with concentration as if posing for a famous sculptor.

Leila turned back around and watched as the young man with the key disappeared through the gate, locked it behind him, then came back through and locked it behind him again. He did this three times, then sat and looked at nothing in particular. The woman in the light blue cardigan touched Leila's arm.

'Your man not show up as yet?'

Leila shook her head, glad of the excuse to talk with someone.

'I shouldn't worry if I was you. He bound to show up. He can't forget a thing like going to England. I mean, how it going look tomorrow morning when he wake up and have to explain to people that yesterday night he get so drunk that he clean forget he supposed to be accompanying his wife and child to England. How you think he going feel if he have to do that?'

12

She sucked her teeth. 'I tell you how he going feel. He going feel like a fool and there don't be no man yet born who can deal with feeling like a damn fool.'

Leila smiled, but she worried. She could feel her heart stabbing against her ribs. Sure that it must be keeping Calvin awake, she held him off slightly. The woman in the light blue cardigan took this as an invitation to liberate the child from his mother's arms.

'Why you not tell me the boy making you feel tired? Here, let me take him and you just sit yourself down.'

Leila hesitated, then crouched, naked without child, on the elegant brown leather suitcase (no address being advertised) that she had bought especially for the journey. She watched as the woman hugged her son too close and rocked him too violently, but she avoided Calvin's abandoned stare. She was happy to be relieved of his weight, if only for a few minutes, and she closed her eyes. Her head began to feel heavy and inattentive, and despite her worries Leila could feel herself falling asleep. All she could do now was hope that her son would be safe.

This morning the seemingly restless sun had risen particularly early, or so it had seemed to Leila. She had left Michael asleep in bed and begun to do the packing. She washed and changed Calvin and made him something to eat before Millie arrived. Then she woke Michael up and got him out of the house so that Millie and herself could start packing up the things in the bedroom. Leila felt tired and she was unable to disguise it from Millie. In fact she did not even bother to try. They left the bedroom and went into the other room. Leila paused. She was perspiring like a cane-cutter.

'You feeling alright?'

Leila did not answer.

'You should rest up a minute.'

Leila peered over her friend's shoulder and out through the

almost permanently open door. Across the road the naked children bathed under the rusty stand-pipe which dribbled water on to their boneless limbs. They splashed and played the best they could. It was already a clear, hot day.

'What happen if you get sick on the ship, or boat, or whatever it is you going on?'

Leila wiped her forehead.

'I'm just tired, that's all. It'll be alright.'

'It'll be alright,' mimicked Millie. 'It'll be alright when you done kill your arse dead.'

Leila turned and withdrew to the bedroom. Millie sighed deeply, then followed her.

The sun burned furiously and high. It was afternoon. They both moved back into the front room where it was cooler. Millie found less and less to do, so she stayed relatively quiet and held the sleeping Calvin as if he were her own child. And Leila packed then unpacked the new suitcase, unable to decide exactly what it was they would need in England. She stopped and thought. Millie had made up some soft drinks, and Leila opened two bottles and passed one to Millie. Millie drank and spat. She did not like grapefruit. She had brought the grapefruit drinks for Leila to take on the ship. Leila said nothing. She reached for a lemon drink, opened it and passed it over. Millie tipped up the bottle to her mouth, swilled it around, tested it thoroughly making sure it really was lemon, then swallowed and spoke.

'Why is it that white people do behave so funny?'

Leila heard the question. 'Do they?'

Millie paused for a moment. 'But I don't know for real though, do I? It's just what I seeing around these parts.'

Leila picked up a light cotton skirt. Millie looked at her.

'You mad at me for I don't mean your father, you know.'

Leila folded the skirt and somehow managed to press it into the suitcase. She took the child from Millie. Calvin had a powerful grip and he clung tightly to his mother's

14

blouse, pinching the shallow skin around her breasts.

'Of course I'm not mad with you.'

Millie avoided her friend's eyes. She reached out, picked up the wrong bottle and took a drink. This time she did not spit it out. She swallowed hard.

By the time Leila had finished the packing, and the one suitcase was full, it was past five o'clock. They sat together on the doorstep and searched for a moment's peace. They could see the clouds quickening as they moved across the mountain tops, and all around them life in the usually noisy street seemed prematurely spent. The night before, Leila had decided that if England was going to be a new start after the pain of the last year, then she must take as little as possible with her to remind her of the island. What she left Millie was to have. What Millie did not want would be left in the house for the new owners to do with what they wanted. And now it was almost time to leave. Leila had spent the whole day packing just one suitcase, trying to define an old life and a new one within the pitiful confines of three feet by two feet by nine inches. She felt sad and stole a sideways glance at Millie. This afternoon they had talked, but not about anything of consequence. They had both felt time's pressure dull their conversation.

Leila stood up. They looked at each other, then at the suitcase, then at each other again. They did not want to reminisce. That would exclude the future. Yet they could not speculate together about what was to come, for, at this moment, their lives seemed destined to take radically different paths. Best friends, closer than sisters for all of their nineteen years, this final afternoon they had almost become strangers. In the brightness of the morning, with the departure still far enough away for this day to be like any other, they had talked. Leila's tiredness, her fears for her mother's health, Millie's pregnancy, white women in England; but now the arched movement of the sun had built a gate through which only one of them could pass.

They fed the suitcase on to a small wooden trolley and began the journey together, with Leila carrying the baby and Millie pulling the trolley. Above them they heard the rusty, troubled cry of a small flock of gulls.

The late afternoon was still hot, and the heat rose up causing the air to shimmer and the people and houses to vibrate. They walked the two hundred yards around the bend in the dusty road and stood out of sight of the village. They were alone, and they waited like refugees fleeing from the front-line of some war-torn country. Millie played nervously with the trolley. Beneath her feet she could feel the dry baked earth full of yawning cracks. She kicked at a little dust and watched with infantile fascination as the cloud settled and coloured her foot a lighter, sandier brown.

Leila looked across at the lonely structure of Frances Gumb's house. She smiled sadly to herself, seeing the sign of a Christian-inspired endeavour. Beside the house someone had tried to scratch a garden into the dust, but the baffled shrubs lay rootless on the beaten hardness of the ground.

When the bus for the capital arrived, the driver and another man who was sitting near the front loaded on the suitcase and trolley for them. The journey continued. The bus crashed down the narrow lane, veering crazily like a drunk. As always, Leila had the sensation that the brakes had failed, but today she did not mind. The speed at which the outside world passed by the window reduced life to a blur; this reflected her own desire to erase from her mind all memory of the last year. Nothing was allowed to remain in focus, all was either too distant or too close, unrecognizable, soon past and forgotten.

Once in the capital they made their way down to the quayside where the queue for the midnight ship had already begun to form. Leila took her place behind the young woman who would later put on a light blue cardigan. The woman stood by a huge cardboard box which was covered over by a white linen sheet. Even though the address was not visible

Leila knew that beneath the shroud some anxious hand would have already painted on the destination.

The ship lay offshore, waiting. She had lain at anchor a week and presumably she had rusted a little since then. Leila watched as she rusted a little further and waited for her cargo.

'It looks quite a nice ship,' observed Millie.

A shiver ran through Leila as the sea breeze pierced the humid air.

'Big. It's big,' added Millie.

Leila felt Calvin's forehead. He was sweating lightly. She wrapped her mother's bright orange shawl around her shoulders and trapped Calvin in the warmth between her breasts. She looked down at Millie. They were entering an autumnal phase which was painful for them both. Millie, small, black, radiant, a woman living in a little girl's body, smiled and her eyes shone out into the night. Millie began to talk incessantly to stop herself crying. Her best friend was leaving. Eventually Leila touched her.

'I'll be alright now. Michael will soon be here and you better be getting back to collect Shere.'

Millie's lips parted but her mouth would not work. Leila did not want them to remember each other as embarrassed by the other's presence. Millie seemed to understand and needed no persuasion. She fought hard, trying not to blink so that the tears in her eyes would not spill out on to her cheeks. She hugged Leila tightly, then Calvin softly. Feeling uncomfortable, they merely stared at each other. Then Millie spoke.

'Till whenever, then.'

'Till whenever, Millie.'

'Say so long to Michael for me and tell Bradeth I'm waiting.'

Millie hovered dangerously. Leila could not answer. She smiled, and after another pause Millie broke the spell and left. She was crying bravely and openly.

An hour later the woman in front began to talk to Leila and tell her all about her husband in England. Leila tried not to listen. Behind her more people joined the queue and it disappeared around the customs house.

Leila opened her eyes and took her son from the woman in the light blue cardigan. The woman said nothing and her face just ached with a desire for sleep as Leila's must have done an hour or so earlier. Leila felt guilty for leaving Calvin with her for so long. Then the young man with the key went through the gate and came back to sit, whistle and stare. This time he stared directly at Leila with the malign benevolence of a judge about to pass sentence. She looked upwards and away. Against the deep blue-black sky the African breadfruit trees towered, sunburnt in the daylight, charcoal-black at night, proud of their history. They were brought here to feed the slaves. They were still feeding them. They would not feed Calvin.

The light breeze dropped, stiffened, then changed direction.

It was almost midnight when Leila heard their voices, loud and discordant, like a brass band at a wake.

'I know it's the boat, man. I can see it, you know. I got two eyes in me head which is more than I can say for the arse who umpire the game last year. How a man can give me out leg before to me Bradman stroke?'

'Leg side ball, man. Leg side,' confirmed Bradeth.

'They too much cheat. Too much frigging cheat.'

They were at the customs house end of the queue.

Leila turned away and watched as the young man again opened the gate. This time he did not go through. He whispered something to the young couple at the front and made a sign to the rest by waving his arms. In the scramble to pick up luggage and shake off sleep there was a smaller scramble as Michael and Bradeth spotted Leila and pushed their way towards her.

'I see you get a good place,' began Michael.

18

Leila stepped forward but said nothing. She left the suit-case for Michael to carry.

'Lemme take the thing, nuh,' offered Bradeth.

'So what happen? You coming England too?'

Bradeth pulled at the suitcase. 'Not this trip, sir, not this trip.' He was out of breath. 'But you all going be seeing me soon for I coming to seek me fortune.'

Michael rescued the suitcase from Bradeth's tentative grip, then he dropped it on his own foot.

'Me arse!' he screamed.

'No man, you is arse,' observed Bradeth, 'and arse is arse, but is you foot you drop the thing on.'

Leila moved out of sight, and Michael had little option but to follow. He was in danger of losing the place he had never really claimed.

'I check you soon, man,' shouted Bradeth.

'Not if I check you sooner.'

Michael left, and Bradeth hopped from foot to foot, wan-ting to cry. It had all happened too quickly.

On the way out to the ship Michael and the suitcase sat at the opposite end of the small boat to Leila and the baby. Leila managed to get Calvin to close his eyes and she looked across at Michael. Like his son, he seemed ready to sleep. She looked past his head and back towards the island of their birth. The bright semi-circle of the capital was reflected in the water like an elaborate candelabra. But she was leaving all this behind. While the dew prepared to dampen the earth and the crickets cried out, she was leaving. And a hundred yards from the shore, in the already greying attic of her West Indian mind, the island was beginning to look small.

Once on board the ship she helped her drunken husband lie down in the small metallic cabin. He cleared his throat and scratched his nose like a dog having a bad dream. Then she laid Calvin on the top bunk. Leila tried to peer out of the porthole but could see only half the island. She moved quickly. The fluff and dust swirled across the floor.

On deck she saw the ferry boats were still carrying their emigrants. But soon it would all be over. This small proud island, overburdened with vegetation and complacency, this had been her home. She looked, feeling sorry for those satisfied enough to stay. Then she stiffened, ashamed of what she had just thought. Then she relaxed again.

In the distance she imagined she could make out the figures of a woman and a small child. She knew it would be Beverley and the baby, but it did not matter now. Leila went downstairs to her cabin and undressed in the darkness so as not to disturb her husband and her son. Then she climbed up and lay down beside Calvin and waited.

Hours later, while the others slept, it happened. The ship lurched forward, then backward, then forward again, towards England. But Leila was still awake and worrying. She listened to the useless tune of the sea and thought of her mother.

HOME

'Michael?' asked Millie, her voice shrill with disbelief. 'On time? You sure we talking about the same man?'

A year earlier Leila had stepped down into the evening gloom. She looked left, then right, but there was no sign of either of them approaching. Behind her the wooden offices which made up the Government headquarters, a two-storey verandahed building, always freshly painted and well-maintained, had long since closed for the night. Leila worked in this impressive structure which, given the one-storeyed ubiquity of the capital's other buildings, towered new, a monument to progress.

Millie, small and spidery, scratched about at the top of the steps. She looked bored and restless as if sheltering from rain, and as ever she wore a plain white skirt and a green khaki shirt (two or three sizes too big). Her choice of colours seemed to make her already black skin look even blacker. And the day's heat left a shiny gloss on her body which would, as the night darkened, first catch, then reflect the light from the moon. Millie, with her bushy-up hair, which to comb posed problems similar to those of a man trying to erect a tent in a hurricane, was more attractive than pretty. A small black girl-woman.

'I don't know why you acting so worry for. You know where the two of them going be.'

Leila listened, then pushed her hands deep into the front pockets of her apron-like skirt and shrugged her shoulders. Michael had never pretended to being the punctual sort of man but Leila's mind could not come to terms with the irrationality of expecting him to be so. Like a teacher trying to cajole a gifted but wayward child, she wanted him to care about such things more than he actually did. Leila continued to wait patiently, but Millie could take no more.

'I sure if he get Santa Claus job he not going turn up till February done and gone.' She sucked her teeth. 'And Bradeth just the blasted same.'

Leila moved, and her slow shadow lengthened and crossed the street. Millie came down the steps towards her.

'Well come, nuh. Let's go. There's no point in standing here like it's World War Three we waiting for.'

Michael and Bradeth had been sitting and drinking for hours. They were both tired. Bradeth drew a line in the dusty road with his big toe but it was not the straight line that he had hoped for. He could not be bothered to try again. He lay back, hands behind his head, and rested against the cool but bumpy wooden slats which made up the whitewashed façade of the Day to Dawn bar. Michael watched him do this. Then he looked at the crooked line and saw that his friend had failed. He could not complain. He would not be trying himself. He wore shoes.

It was after five and still hot and humid; people shuffled and ambled their way up and down the main street. Michael took his eyes from them and again he looked across at Bradeth who had secretly taken the precaution of pulling down a straw hat over his face to block out the sun. His gawky body jutted out from all directions and it was clear why many saw Bradeth as more giraffe than man. He did not sit, he collapsed. And when he walked he strode. From his elbows outwards and from his knees downwards, all coordination, all bodily harmony, seemed beyond his powers of control. Yet there was a loping beauty about his unique body, the head small and pecking like that of a bird, his eyes bright and restless. A dog hopped over Bradeth's legs and without looking back it skipped on carelessly up the street and around the corner and out of sight. It seemed to know where it was going.

Michael tipped up a bottle of beer, drained it in one and tossed it away to his left. He straightened his bright pink shirt and tucked it into his pants. Even when there was no reason to dress up well he liked to maintain a neat and tidy appearance. Being of medium height and build, he was lucky in that almost everything fitted him. However, if a shirt was too short in the sleeves he would concentrate hard so as to remember not to lift up his arms away from his sides unless it was strictly necessary, and if the sleeves were too long he would carefully turn back both cuffs, just the one fold. He leaned forward and his right hand found the black leather shoe on his right foot. For a few moments he worked away, vigorously scraping off some dried mud from the heel, then he licked his fingers and cleaned up the smears. If Bradeth had bothered to put on some long pants instead of his usual shorts, he would have polished up the shoe against Bradeth's trousers and risked waking him up. He could not subject his own pants to such treatment.

A school bus crept down the road and the children pressed their round faces up against the windows. Michael stared back at them. Behind the bus a cloud of slow dust, seemingly disinclined to rise up from the road, began to mask the lingering sight. Michael watched as the bus eventually disappeared from view.

'Man, you sleeping or what?' he asked, without turning his head.

Bradeth remained motionless. He waited a moment, then replied, 'Who you calling sleeping?'

'Who you think it is I calling sleeping? King of England?'

'Me not sleeping, boy. I just resting up me head a little.'

'So what happen? You can't take your beer?'

Bradeth sucked his teeth and spat. The transparent globular mess nestled down on the surface of the road. It vibrated slightly. Unlike water, it was not going to evaporate. Michael eyed it suspiciously before stretching out his foot and grinding it into the dust so that only a damp brown patch remained. Then he turned to Bradeth.

'Maybe you should take up your arse and go back to work.'

Again Bradeth sucked his teeth.

'Who you talking to about work? The day I see you take up a job is the day you can talk with me about going back to work.'

Michael listened, then thought for a moment, then spoke, as if trying to convince himself of something.

'I has a job for I thought you and me was partners for true.'

Bradeth chuckled, his face gently parting to reveal his white teeth. His shoulders began to ripple in comic disbelief.

'Partners?' he asked. 'You and me, partners?'

Michael opened another bottle of beer and Bradeth went on, his whole body now shaking with laughter.

'You do a few deliveries for me round the back of the island and that make you a partner?' He opened his eyes. 'You know I never did understand you, man, for sometimes you do act funny and say some damn foolishness.'

Michael turned away and took a silent drink. He looked across the street at nothing in particular, just a row of wooden planked shop fronts, now all closed up and bolted for the night. In the bar behind him he heard somebody punch a quarter into the machine and an old calypso began to play. Unconsciously they both began to follow the tune and they switched off from each other. Then, like Michael's, Bradeth's eyes also drifted across the street, searching first one way, then the next, eagerly awaiting signs of early evening life.

The tune ended and they listened as the disc clicked back into place. The barman switched on the radio. Bradeth brushed up against Michael as he gestured towards the unopened bottles.

'Pass me one of them nuh, man.'

Michael tossed a bottle to his friend.

'Thank you, man.' Bradeth took a deep swig. 'Ahh! Life can be good.'

Michael turned to him. 'You think so?'

Bradeth held back from taking the next swig.

'What it is eating you up, man?' He paused for a moment then went on, 'We can't really classify as partners for it's me who do all the work. You just run a few deliveries on your bike and that is all.'

'I not talking about partners still,' snapped Michael.

He stood up and felt his bones creak. He stretched, pushing his arms skywards, and rolled forwards on to the balls of his feet. Then the tension rushed from his body and he fell backwards and flat on to the thin soles of his shoes.

'I have to piss.'

Michael moved around the side of the bar and propped himself up, one palm resting against the zinc fence. He encouraged his urine to thunder noisily against the metal.

'What I'm talking about is the goodness of life. You say life is good.'

He carefully dripped himself off and strolled back around the corner to take up his place. He shuffled as he sat, trying to rediscover his exact position. Bradeth let him settle before resuming the conversation.

'Well, what is wrong with you, man, for you having a nice time sitting out in the sun, drinking beer, listening to music and talking. What else it is you want?' Bradeth took a drink and carried on. 'And you have motorbike standing up there that everyone admire you for.'

Michael sucked his teeth and in one swig emptied his bottle. He threw it to one side.

Bradeth continued, 'And in two days you going be marrying to one of the finest looking girls on the island and you questioning me about if life can be good. Beer done lick you down?'

Michael looked up to where the stars would soon be.

'It's not that easy, you know. It's not that easy.'

Bradeth put down his now empty bottle. 'You mean because

27

of Beverley and the child?'

'Maybe,' said Michael.

Bradeth went on, 'I sure she know about that. Women not stupid, you know.'

He paused, then Michael spoke. 'I don't think it going make no difference anyway, so I'm not worrying.'

Again Bradeth spat. 'So what it is you moaning about?'

Michael shrugged his shoulders. They sat together in silence, depression rolling in over them. Whatever they said they now seemed destined to argue.

Michael went back inside for two more bottles and they drank them. Then, in the twilight, they fell asleep, slumped up against each other. The dust in the road was allowed to settle as fewer cars and even fewer bicycles passed by. Only the Day to Dawn bar, and Jumbies rum bar down the other end of the street remained open. Those who persisted in town were inside one of the two bars and only a few stragglers and fishermen hung about outside. In the distance the sun slipped unobserved and lonely into the cold sea.

Leila, the taller and lighter of the two girls, obediently followed her friend as they walked purposefully to the end of the street and around the corner by Jumbies rum bar. There they both faltered and listened to the smoky noises leaking through the closed shutters and underneath the crooked door. Outside a drunk body lay bulky in the road, like a sack of sugar that had inadvertently slipped off the back of a lorry. They walked on.

Even from this distance it was clear that the men were both asleep. They approached, Leila feeling much the more foolish for having encouraged Millie to spend a hopeful, wasted hour outside Government House while knowing in her heart that neither Bradeth nor Michael would come. She lagged behind a little.

Millie pushed Bradeth's shoulder and he shook himself away from Michael. Then Michael's somnolent head fell quickly, but he woke before it made contact with the ground.

'You both have a nice sleep, then?' asked Millie, her hands firmly on her hips.

The men rubbed their eyes and stretched. Bradeth explained, 'We just decided to take a nap and check out what a bit of peace and quiet feel like, but it's not looking like we going finish the test.'

'I see,' said Millie. 'Well, now that the testing done maybe you don't mind testing your backside up to Sandy Bay with me where my aunt wants to have a word with you about something.'

Bradeth moved to get up. 'Toosie?'

'It's only one aunt I has in Sandy Bay, or maybe you hear of a next one.'

'I just checking, that's all.' Bradeth stood, hind legs first, and reached up to hold his head straight.

'So you get hangover as well?' asked Millie.

'It's just a little headache that I had for a long time now,' said Bradeth. 'A long time now.'

'I know,' said Millie. 'Since when you begin to drink is about how long you had it. You coming or what?'

Bradeth sucked his teeth and dusted down his shorts. Millie turned to Leila.

'I going call round later and let you know what happen.'

'Alright,' said Leila.

Millie pulled sharply at Bradeth's shirt, which was flapping in the breeze. He seized it from her.

'What the hell is all this mystery nonsense?' He tucked his own shirt tail back into his shorts. 'And what it is you going let she know later on?' Millie pushed her finger into Bradeth's chest.

'Bradeth, please just shut up your mouth and let we go for I done spend enough time waiting for your backside to appear.' He did not move. 'Come!' shouted Millie. 'Come before I box you one lick!'

Carefully avoiding his eyes, Bradeth nodded Michael a final farewell. He fell in one step behind Millie. Leila watched as the pair of them, one oversized, one undersized, marched off to try and find a stray taxi or bus, anything that would take them to the country. They soon became silhouettes.

Michael moved to get up.

'I'm sorry I didn't meet you, but I just forget and fall asleep.' Leila brushed off some dust from his sleeve.

'Well, I found you anyway.' She stood on her tiptoes, put her hands on his shoulders, and kissed him lightly on the lips. It was not that he was that much taller than her, but she knew he liked it when she stretched to reach him.

'I better get back home,' said Leila, 'for I have a lot of things to get sorted out with my mother.' She paused. 'And I have to read to her.'

'Tonight?' asked Michael. Leila nodded.

He took her hands from his shoulders and moved across the street to the motorbike. She followed, got on and hooked her arms tightly around his waist. Michael kicked the starter and a few people began to drift out of the Day to Dawn bar. He raced the engine, filling the air with a thick smoke, then he took off, violently weaving his way down the twenty or thirty yards to the end of the street. Once there he braked, threw the bike to his right, and straightened up before accelerating up the west coast toward St Patrick's. The spectators wandered back inside the bar and again there was silence in Baytown.

As the island rushed past, Leila held her head back and let the wind play with her hair. To her left lay the sea, which gently lapped up the beach before stopping and spreading back upon itself; to her right lay a bed of vegetation which swam out flat and expansive until it brushed into the first heavy slopes of the mountains. Leila shifted her view from left to right, then back to the left and so on, enjoying the freedom that she always felt when riding on the back of the bike. But Michael remained stiff, slamming the bike into curve after curve, choosing the most frenzied rhythms of the road.

As they swept through Sandy Bay Leila looked for Toosie's shop, which lay a little way off the road, but she could see that only a small light was burning. Obviously Millie and Bradeth had not yet arrived. Then she remembered. They had passed neither taxi nor bus and Leila was sure that Toosie would be irritable, idly squinting into the candlelight and waiting for them both.

As they left Sandy Bay Leila waved at some children, and they waved back eagerly. They should have been in bed, she thought, for it was dark now. And then the low vegetation to her right was immediately replaced with the familiar high fencing of sugar cane. Sometimes the road between Sandy Bay and St Patrick's was fenced in on one side, sometimes on both, sometimes neither, but more often than not the mountain side of the road offered no view and it was like riding through a partially constructed tunnel. Then the engine began to cough and splutter. It threatened to die, but as it neared the last gasp Michael managed to revive it and nurse it back to health.

He pulled up outside her mother's house and Leila slipped off the bike. He spoke quickly. 'I see you Saturday, then.'

Leila nodded her reply, and Michael spun the bike around and disappeared into the mouth of the bend. He did not even smile. Long after he had gone the noise of the engine still seemed to hum in her head. Leila waited a few minutes, then it was quiet again. She should have been home a long time ago to read to her mother, for the day after tomorrow she would be married. Then, more wife than daughter, she would no longer have time for stories.

Her mother sat as if courting misery. There were no pictures on the bare walls, no carpets on the wooden floors, and at the back of a long, thin room stood two attentive doors. The door to the left led into Leila's room, the door to the right into her mother's, but in this one rectangular room they cooked, ate, talked and read. This was the way it had been for as long as Leila could remember, and this was the way it would be as long as they were just mother and daughter. In front of her mother an uneasy pile of books rested on a small circular table. The present book lay on top, face down, leaves spread wide like a square butterfly come to rest.

She was, unlike her only child, a dark, almost black woman and she spoke with a deep voice. She could no longer shout, her body having been steadily eroded by an illness which left her looking much older than her forty years. Though her high cheekbones suggested the skeletal, in her proud voice one could detect the lost joy of a voluptuous past. For her this was no longer life as she just stumbled from day to day.

'Where have you been and I don't want any sideways tale.'

As she said this she bent slowly and reached under her chair, picking up a prayerbook from off the floor. Leila followed her every move. Her mother was not a religious woman and it confused her. She straightened up and felt for the secure support of her stick.

'Here, take it.'

She thrust the book upon her daughter. There was silence. Leila fumbled with the prayerbook and avoided her mother's stare.

'Child, I'm waiting.'

Leila faltered as she spoke, her voice breaking with every syllable.

'I left work at the normal time and Millie came to meet me. Then we waited for Bradeth and Michael but they did not come, so we went to find them.' She stopped and dared to look at her mother whose face was icily attentive.

'Where you find them?'

Leila lowered her voice. 'Day to Dawn.' Her mother picked up her cue.

'Go on.'

'And then Michael drove me home.'

32

'And that is all?' Leila nodded. 'It take you so long to get back here?'

Again Leila nodded. Her mother left the room quietly. She closed the door behind her, and Leila stood alone in the semi-darkness.

It was the night Michael had walked all the way from Sandy Bay to St Patrick's, to ask for an answer to his proposal, that things between Leila and her mother had really started to go wrong.

Her mother had lain in bed, the sheet pulled up to her neck, which made her appear grotesque, as if she were merely a dismembered head resting upon a clean white pillow. Leila had sat on the edge of her bed as if visiting a patient in hospital. Her mother looked up at her, then closed her eyes.

'So when he ask you to marry to him?'

'Today, this evening,' whispered Leila.

'So what you done with your reasonings?' she asked.

Leila said nothing.

Her mother went on, 'You think he is the man to make you happy? You think he is something that Arthur don't be?'

Leila listened, then spoke cautiously. 'I love Michael, I don't love Arthur.'

'And you think it's that simple?' She opened her eyes and looked into her daughter's face. 'You cold?' she asked. Leila nodded for all she had on was a loose shift. Having finally plucked up courage she had crawled out of bed and come into her mother's room as she was. She had not even pulled on a gown.

'So what you going do?'

Leila lowered her eyes. 'I want to marry to him.'

'But I asked you what you going do?' Her mother paused. 'You can't tell me?'

Leila parted her lips, though they clung to each other until the last possible moment.

'I want your advice.'

'I see, so it's my advice you come seeking?' Leila tried to smile. Her mother shook her head. 'You going write Arthur and tell him?'

Leila nodded. 'I'll write and tell him.'

Her mother sighed, long and hard. 'You're a fool, girl. A damn fool and you let me down. Arthur is a good man and the boy from Sandy Bay is no good. He loves himself too much and he will use you. He don't even have a job.' She looked at her daughter who was close to tears. 'If you don't see that, girl, then you don't see nothing and I don't bring up no blind child.' She paused, half-exhausted, half-frustrated. 'I mean, why a girl like you want to marry to such a man? I just don't understand.'

There was a long silence and Leila knew her mother had finished. She was being dismissed. Leila got up from the bed and left her mother's room.

She stood alone in the front room, and as the tears began to run down her face she heard a noise outside. Sure that it would be Michael she ran to the door and she could see from the shine on his face that he had been running. But she could also see that he had been listening. Michael threw the flowers at her feet and before she could stoop to pick them up he spat on them. Leila felt the cold spit trickling down the slope of her foot. She looked up and caught his eyes with hers. Then she rushed forward and threw out her arms, but it was like hugging a statue. As she thudded against him he rocked back slightly. His arms did not move from his side nor his feet from the earthly pedestal they were rooted to. He was stable, and lifeless, and balanced.

'Michael, I'll marry you.'

Michael turned and left without speaking to her.

From that night, things between Leila and her mother changed, but Michael too began to behave differently. Before that night, he used occasionally to comment on how good she looked and bring her the odd small gift, but somewhere at the back of her mind Leila felt that, unlike Arthur, he had never really known how to do these things. He had simply been remembering that he ought to be doing them. After that night he began to forget, and although he had said nothing, Michael no longer appeared to be trying.

There was a light tapping at the door. Leila jumped, a little frightened at first, then she made her way across the room and let Millie in.

'What happened?' asked Millie hurriedly.

'Nothing,' said Leila. 'She was angry that I was late.'

'But you tell her that they never show up?'

'Yes.'

'And what?'

'And nothing.'

'I see.' said Millie. 'So you not read for her?' Leila shook her head and there was a long pause as Millie looked around at the familiar drabness.

Leila lit the lamp.

'I'm tired,' said Millie.

Leila thought for a moment before replying, 'Me too.'

Leila picked up the lamp and led the way to her bedroom where they both got undressed and crawled into bed beside each other. They spoke in a whisper, Millie first. 'You tell her I going spend the night here?'

Leila lied because she knew it would be alright. 'I told her. It's alright.'

'Good.' Leila gave Millie half the pillow and they settled down. Then Leila spoke. 'What happen with you?'

Millie made herself comfortable. 'Just what I tell you would happen. Before we get to my Aunt Toosie's house I just tell Bradeth I pregnant and he don't say anything like his ears done fall off he small head.'

'You mean he didn't say anything?'

35

'He don't say a damn thing. Then I tell him I going have to tell my aunt for she going find out sooner or later and he just say "yes", like it's 10 cents I ask him to borrow.'

'Is that all?'

'That's all. So when we get to she place and I tell her, and she say that he should marry to me if he be any kind of man at all, you never guess what he do next.' Millie paused dramatically, but she gave Leila no time to hazard an answer. 'The man get up and walk away from the table and auntie shout after him that he should have more blasted manners.'

'So what did you do?'

'I just say "excuse me" and run after him. It's like he be in a dream world. I think the man over-shock. When I catch up with him he just say that he walking back to town to do some thinking. I ask if he going marry to me. He say he don't know but he don't think so but he going support the child.' Leila wanted to interrupt but she let Millie go on.

'So I go back and tell my aunt this and she say it's better than nothing.' Millie paused for a moment, then went on, 'You know the man shock. Sort of lost for true.'

'You don't care that he's not going to marry to you?' asked Leila, her face creased with worry. Millie looked at her friend, then smiled.

'He going marry to me,' she said. 'Just wait and see. He going marry to me soon enough.'

Leila reached over a tired hand and turned out the lamp. She wanted to know one more thing. They lay in darkness now.

'Do you love Bradeth?' asked Leila.

Millie giggled. 'It's a stupid question, for course I love the man. It's the most important bit, you know.'

Leila thought for a moment. 'I suppose it is,' she said. 'I just wanted to make sure.'

Next door Leila's mother was asleep but her sickly cough still polluted the night. Leila listened and wondered if she was going to be alright. But she convinced herself that she would be. Millie turned and lay on her back, hands by her side, mouth slightly open. She fell asleep. Leila watched as occasionally she snored and sniffed. Then Leila listened to her mother coughing and tried to fall asleep.

Like Leila, Michael slept badly. He awoke as mature daylight streamed in under the door and he guessed that it must be nearly midday. For a moment he was confused. Normally he was awake by 8 o'clock at the latest, it being too hot to stay in bed any later. Then he remembered. Last night. The memories were not pleasant so he lay down again. He closed his eyes and pulled the sheet up over his head.

He was in the pious atmosphere of his grandmother's house. He could hear her out on the front step listening to one of the American radio stations which broadcast religious programmes all day long. He visualized her with the accuracy of a freshly drying photograph. She was a stout woman with a deep black face, a face so old that it looked like it had been partly melted by years of exposure to the sun; shapeless, like a fused tyre. Her eyes were small, her nose only vaguely prominent, her lips almost invisible and the colour of the rest of her skin. He knew she would be squinting into the sun, only closing her eyes when they could no longer drink any more of the good Lord's light. It was in this rêverie that she best liked to listen to the sinners being consumed in burning lakes, to the ominous voices from the clouds, repentance, donations, forgiveness, and then the clearly annunciated post office box number in Salt Lake City. Michael heard her beginning to hum to the clear strains of a lonely hymn and he decided to leave her to the serenity she deserved. He would not get up. She had probably not heard him come in last night but no doubt she had already looked to make sure that he was here this morning. This being the case they both knew where the other was, and what they were doing, and they liked it that way. Michael let sleep steal back into his body.

Last night only the thin sound of water lapping up against the beach had disturbed the calm, but it was a night of hidden eyes. A quiet, mysterious night, and in the far distance a dog sat on its haunches and bayed at the moon. Michael had only travelled about half a mile back down the road towards Sandy Bay when the bike's engine had finally spluttered and given up. Fortunately the road was flat, so after the engine cut out he let the bike cruise for a hundred yards before its momentum finally faded and he was forced to rest his feet on the ground. He got off, wheeled it over to the side of the road and kicked the stand underneath it. Michael's first thought was to wait for a car to pass and take a lift into Sandy Bay, but he did not want to leave the bike. So, with one hand pushed into his trouser pocket, he waited. He looked down the empty road to where St Patrick's lay, but he knew he would not go back there tonight. He could probably beg, borrow or steal a bicycle for the night, but he did not want to risk the possibility of bumping into Leila. He would see her on Saturday. He leaned against the bike and looked out over the cane to the sea. Above him the trees made hesitating, whimpering sounds, and as he listened a great moth blundered into his face, then curled away into the night. If he had been a smoker he would have smoked. He just thought and waited.

It would have been different, he thought, if he had a car, but as far as he could see there was no chance of his ever having that kind of big money. He had no qualifications. Being thirteen when his grandfather had died he had little choice but to leave school. The few pennies he could scratch selling country fruit in the town or, when the time came, weeding the fields, had made more sense to his grandmother than money spent on his books and uniform. (Perhaps she was right, for you could not buy a car with a school certificate. It took a different sort of paper. His grandfather had taught him that.) Which left only cricket. If you did not make it at school, they said, you had to make it with the bat. But Michael was not displaying any flair in this sphere either, and he realized this and sold the bat his grandfather had made for him. With the 40 cents he bought his first beer. To celebrate he dropped his voice, then he learned how to walk slowly, like a man, then he learned how to spit and curse.

He arrived home drunk and found his grandfather sitting up waiting for him, the glow from a firing candle lighting up his face. With his eyes he silently beckoned his grandson to come and sit opposite him. As he did so he squinted, as if in old age he was beginning to see life through a plate of frosted glass. Young Michael sat nervously and watched his grandfather scratch at his thick arm where strength still slept, then slowly rub the palm of his hand over the stubborn and hard hair on his greying head. His hands were knotted, his teeth gappy and yellow. Like aged tombstones they sloped backwards. Somehow Michael knew his grandfather was about to die and that what he had to say would be important. In the corner stood his grandmother. She stared at Michael, a small giddy boy in short pants, slumped, trying to sit straight, and her face was heavy with disapproval. Michael avoided her eyes, waited for his grandfather and listened. The wind rattled the door and he knew it would soon rain.

'So you sell the bat?' Michael nodded, mystified as to how his grandfather knew. 'Well, I glad.'

His grandfather spoke as if conducting a funeral. 'This island too full of old men who telling you how good they used to be, and how they nearly open at Lords one time, and all kinds of stupidness, and all they has to show for it is a piece of wood and an empty belly.' He paused. 'At least you don't going have the piece of wood and you already had the sense to buy some drink to put in you belly.' His grandfather's voice began to falter a little but he went on, 'You don't look to me like the type of boy who going to die in the arms of a white man.' He let out a low crumbling laugh, then stopped abruptly. 'But you might.' He paused. 'You might, boy, but tonight I going talk to you as a

39

man and if it's man you want to live to be you better listen hard.'

He pushed back his chair and turned to look at his wife. Waving his hand like a slow branch he gestured her out of the room.

'It's man talk.'

As if already briefed for this encounter Michael's grandmother left the men alone. Michael, his blood still rich with drink, looked at his grandfather and barren thoughts chilled his body.

'You don't has no parents, Michael, for my son and your mother did die in the boat almost ten years ago this month, so it's only I can talk to you, and before I dead I going do so or I don't see no way I can have some peace with them in the next world.' He paused, then looked Michael straight in the eyes. He raised his voice.

'Michael, who plant the trees?' Michael shook his head, but his grandfather did not seem to be expecting an answer. 'Yam is Africa man tree, Mango is India man tree, Coconut is Pacific man tree, so who plant the trees, Michael?' He waited a few moments, then lowered his voice to a lilting whisper. 'Who plant the trees, Michael? Who plant them?'

For a few moments they were silent, and in that silence Michael's head spun. The effect of the drink had worn off and it was a different kind of headache, as if a massive hand had reached down out of the ceiling and was clutching him threateningly around the throat. His grandfather's light voice boomed out.

'Among the cane my own father did sire me with neither love nor law, you hear me? Neither love nor law.' He paused. 'I want you to remember this. Next time you see a piece of sugar cane ask yourself when the last time you did see a white man cutting or weeding in the field. I want you to think hard when the last time you did see a white man doing any kind of coloured man work and I want you to remember good.' He

40

paused to catch his breath, then pressed on. 'I don't want you to hate, for I know too well what hate can do. I been doing it for the last sixty odd years and it don't be no good, but I see it in you too much Michael, and you is only a young boy still but you got too much fire in your heart and not enough water in your blood.' Again he paused. He had to think out what he was going to say for he did not want to confuse the boy. So, putting extra weight on every word, he began to speak again, slowly this time.

'You must hate enough, and you must be angry enough to get just what you want but no more! No more! For, if you do, you just going end up hating yourself. Too much laughing is bad for the coloured man, too much sadness is bad for the coloured man, but too much hating is the baddest of them all and can destroy a coloured man for true.' He paused open-mouthed, as if somebody had snatched the words from him. Then he lowered his eyes as if praying. 'It's true.' He looked tired. He had said what he had to say.

Night crept on and they sat looking at each other, communicating silently across the years. An hour passed by. The sky had broken and now the rain was falling steadily. It would go on like this for days. Then the remaining small piece of candle flickered violently and his grandfather's face danced to ghostly life.

'In Costa Rica I never did talk to a white man with my hands in my pockets. Now? Always.' He peeled back his buckled lips and a sly smile creased his face.

'In Panama an old, old man, he can barely pick up an axe, he tell me that the economics of the world be soldered with my sweat. Well, I looking at the man like he crazy or something for all I trying to do is earn two pennies to rub together.' He allowed his smile to break into a laugh. 'Well, boy, it take me nearly forty years to realize that I done meet a prophet, for the economics of the world be soldered with my sweat and your sweat and his sweat and the sweat of every coloured man in the world, you understand?' he asked, his eyes now burning with a near-spent life.

Michael nodded.

'You don't know, boy! You don't know!' He laughed. 'I suppose you also know what I mean when I tell you the West Indies is a dangerous place to be a failure.' Michael nodded again, and his grandfather laughed even louder.

'Ambition going teach you that you going has to flee from beauty, Michael. Panama? Costa Rica? Brazil? America? England? Canada, maybe? West Indian man always have to leave his islands for there don't be nothing here for him, but when you leave, boy, don't be like we. Bring back a piece of the place with you. A big piece. I sick of hearing old men talking about 'When I was in such and such a place', and 'when I was here and there and every damn place', and still they don't has nothing. Ambition going teach you that you going has to flee from beauty and when you gone to wherever, remember me, boy. Remember me.'

The elder of the two men leaned forward and, shielding the little flame of the candle with his cupped hand, he blew out the light and plunged the island into darkness. Outside the gutters raced with water, and the rain drummed out a gentle endless tropical beat on the corrugated iron roof. It was the first bar of a very long song.

Michael saw a car coming towards him, its headlights bouncing like two lost soldiers waving their torches on a lonely road. He dipped out of the light, knelt and pretended to be working on his broken bike. The car rushed past him, his face having been briefly shelled in the glare of the lights. It sounded a friendly horn. Michael had sufficient time to recognize Mr Johnson as the driver and Millie as the passenger. He stood up and watched carefully as the night extinguished the glow of the red tail lights, and again the night was his. Millie was obviously going to stay by Leila tonight. She had probably woken up a tired Mr Johnson so she could take his dollar taxi ride from

Sandy Bay to St Patrick's. Again he leaned against the bike and thought and waited, and this time he fell asleep.

Michael heard the taxi coming back down the road so he quickly stooped and pretended to be still working. The taxi bounced past him throwing up a cloud of dust which crept into his throat. This time Mr Johnson did not sound his horn. Michael coughed, stood up and looked down the road after the car. He had decided. He knocked the bike off its stand and began pushing it the remaining five and a half miles down the road to Sandy Bay. He would not bother going to stay at Beverley's tonight as her house was at the far side of the village. He would stay with his grandmother, that is if he made it back at all, for the bike was not light and the day had already been long.

He began briskly but soon found himself stopping every few hundred yards and looking upwards as he caught his breath. He saw the fireflies speckling the sky with their individual fire, hundreds of them, lights to guide the night flights of restless birds, nature's airport in the sky. Above them the trees watched, like dancers frozen in a fantastic pose, their arms thrown up high over their heads.

By the time Michael woke up his grandmother had fallen asleep. The service over, he could hear her snoring on the front step. He realized that it must be at least six in the evening, for the light no longer streamed in under the door. There was little more than a dull yellow band and the air was heavier and slightly musty. He peeled back the sheet and rolled out of bed into the same long pants and pink shirt that he had worn the previous day. Half of his clothes were here and half were at Beverley's house. He would change there.

His stocky figure presented itself in front of the full-length mirror that covered the inside panel of the wardrobe. The bed apart, it was the only piece of furniture in the room. Michael quickly ran a dull comb backwards across the top of his stubbled head. He pulled on his jacket, stepped out of the bedroom, then crept through the front room and out past his grandmother into the humid air. It was a surprisingly bright evening, the time of the year when days seemed to drag on longer than they should. His bike was still there at the side of the house where he had left it. There seemed little point in even trying to use it. What he needed was a new bike.

Beverley lived ten minutes away, but to get there Michael had to wind his way through a jungle of back streets. Past the old houses made up of sheets of zinc and flattened butter tins nailed together, thatched cane leaf roofs and dirt floors. Past the open bars where on a hungry day if you were lucky, and had 50 cents in your pocket, somebody would sell you a bowl of rice and black-eyed peas, or some vegetables in an oily stew with a piece of bread to dip in it. Past the squatting school-boys, homework done, toasting their feet on the top of the road which, even at this time of day, was still as hot as an oven. They sat with their sugar cane, chew–suck–spit, chew–suck–spit. And past the small girls pushing soursops into their faces, the juice bubbling down their flat naked chests.

An old knotted woman sat and looked, her heavy round breasts fighting against the sweat-stained fabric of her shirt. She was too old for conversation. She could only stare. Her husband, sitting beside her, bony and gnarled, like a twig washed up by the sea, looked up and smiled with both his teeth.

'Crop come, boy. No more weeding, plenty cutting, plenty work.'

The man had known Michael since he was a baby, and if Michael lived to be a hundred years old he would still call him 'boy'. He carried on working, the sharp metallic scratching of cutlass on grinding stone meant that his life had once again taken on some kind of seasonal sense. Michael moved on, too embarrassed to answer.

When he arrived Beverley was preparing Ivor for bed. Michael came in and without saying a word he sat at the table. Beverley put down their child and picked up a pan. She silently spooned some chicken and rice on to a plate and set it before him. Then she carried on putting Ivor into a new nappy.

She was a small, plump woman with a brown skin light enough to be freckled. She had successfully straightened her hair so that it dropped eagerly towards her shoulders. Her husband had left her three years ago to carve out a new life for them both in America, but he had never sent for her. She had everybody's sympathy, though she had no friends. Having recovered from the shock Beverley tried to guarantee herself against further hurt by expecting nothing of this world except a clean house, her child's health and her breath in her body every morning when she woke. Everything else was a complication that could, if necessary, be ignored.

Her house was empty, like the inside of a packing case. It was just one room, with a small bedroom created by a hanging curtain. There were no pictures on the walls, not even one of Jesus, only old calendars. And nothing grew in this home, not even a flower. Behind the curtain stood a low and almost permanently unmade bed. Out back there was a small but clean yard, home for a few thin chickens and a pair of goats that looked more like sick dogs. They wandered aimlessly in between the water tank and the fruit trees, too poor to make any noise.

Michael tossed the chicken leg back on to the plate, having sucked it clean. Ivor's young eyes slid involuntarily across the room, but his mother turned his head and regained his attention. Beverley put the final pin into place and took him across to his father. Michael cradled the boy in his greasy hands. Then, half-heartedly, he touched Ivor's face, but the child began to cry and struggle weakly. They had both had enough. He held the boy up like a bunch of bananas at the market place and waited for a bid. Beverley was the only bidder and she took him, pulled back the curtain, and entered the bedroom space.

Michael pushed the plate away and waited for her to come back out. Sometime ago, when marriage seemed a long way off, he had promised his grandmother that he would spend the night before his wedding at home with her. He would soon have to go. Beverley came back out and carefully pulled the curtain behind her. She turned around and, without looking at Michael, came forward and took up the plate. She put it on the side. Michael followed her with his eyes, knowing that he would simply make love to her, then walk back across the village the way he had come. Prolonged interest in her aroused body was a game he was tired of playing.

He walked quickly. The occasional light was still on but he had to pick his way carefully down the moonlit streets and cut across back gardens and up small alleyways. In his grand-mother's house both lamps were lit. She was waiting. The small wooden shack stood slightly apart from the other houses, and Michael climbed the one step and carefully curled himself around the door.

His attentive grandmother was sitting in her dressing gown, which hid the well-worn cotton nightdress that had grown old with her. Michael stood like a stranger and looked about the room. On a rusty nail behind the door hung her 'burying hat', a hat that looked like an old black felt box that had been crushed out of shape. All her friends were dying. The journey to the door, to the church and back again to the rusty nail was becoming more frequent. Michael waited. Then she creaked slowly to life, pretending she had been asleep, and she looked blankly at him and rolled her tongue around her mouth. She had a full set of upper teeth but her lower jaw contained just three teeth, set at random angles, outcrops of white rock. The middle one jutted out over her bottom lip. But despite her teeth her gums were red and healthy. Sweet, almost succulent.

46

'So what you has to say for yourself now you soon going be married?'

Michael sat opposite her with his back to the front door.

'Don't really be much I can say, is there? It's going to happen and that's all there is to it.'

'If you say so.' She paused for breath. Without taking her eyes from him she went on, 'And what about the Beverley woman and she child? You think about them?' Michael avoided her knowing stare. She carried on, 'Don't worry, I think you is better off with the white girl for she going look after you right if you look after she, you hear me?'

Michael nodded. He looked at his grandmother, then past her and around the room. He saw wisdom and experience not only in her face but in the bundles of letters that were piled up high in boxes and stuffed away in every corner. On the cabinet top were photographs, old, grey, brown, new, bright, of her family, now scattered all over the world, a family she never talked about for she had never seen them. She looked at Michael and forced a smile.

He spoke quickly. 'I think I'll go to bed now.'

They sat in silence for two minutes more, but to Michael it felt like an age. He looked once more at the treasures of her life and thought of his grandfather. He had never noticed before, but without him the house was totally empty. All of a sudden he was missing, gone, and after ten years Michael felt as if he understood his grandmother a little better. He began to feel guilty that it had taken him so long.

He got up, kissed her lightly on the cheek and went through to his room. Michael sat on the bed and listened carefully but he knew his grandmother was going to sit until she thought he was asleep. There would be no Bible tonight. She would spend the whole night praying hard, then sleeping, then praying hard again, and in those moments of consciousness she would listen to make sure that he slept well. He lay back on the bed, hands behind his head, and waited. Now, only hours away from marriage, he thought of Leila.

He always found himself caught between giving to her, and thinking if he was ever going to make anything of his life he would need every last ounce of energy to spend where he chose and when he chose. Sometimes he chose to spend it on her, sometimes not. He had explained this so many times to Bradeth that he began to wonder if his friend was going deaf. It was nothing to do with Beverley, he would say, it was just Leila whom one minute he could like, and the next minute he could look at her filled with a horror that she might betray him in some unknown way. Bradeth usually shrugged, unable to comprehend his friend's slick logic; Michael, however, told him only half the truth.

Most people thought Leila too good for Michael. But he felt that to talk of this with anyone, including Bradeth, was admission to his alleged inferiority. Therefore he kept his anger locked up. This frustrated him, but it also made him more determined to prove something to himself and everyone. What exactly it was he was trying to prove he was still unsure. And how he would prove it he had no idea.

An hour slipped by, and outside he could hear the shrill voices of the crickets. Then he heard the soft ache of wood as his grandmother levered herself out of the chair, and the resigned leathery rustle of her bare feet as she made her way across the empty space to her bedroom. Michael turned over and fell asleep.

*

The next day being Saturday Leila was married. But there was no string band, and nobody danced or sang in the street, and nobody walked with the wedding cake firmly balanced on their head. The service was as her mother had wanted it, strictly

48

Whose convention?

conventional, with Leila dressed from head to foot in a lacy white dress, large raindrop-like earrings in both her ears; and Michael looking smart in a dark blue suit, a white shirt and a tie. He had made an effort, and it showed. Leila was grateful.

Inside Sandy Bay Anglican Church the walls bulged at their seams for, as ever on these occasions, there were too many guests. It soon became very hot. The congregation began to fan themselves, softly at first, then with a greater vigour as the minutes grew longer and the service more trying. Leila stood rigid, frightened to move, or blink, or smile even. Outside the church row upon row of well-wishers waited patiently, slowly burning in the midday sun, their sticky bodies pressed up warmly, but without invitation, against each other. Michael was a poor boy from this village and he was marrying the mulatto girl from St Patrick's. He had done well for himself and they waited with anxiety. Even if it took all day they would wait; if nothing else, the marriage had been announced in heavy capitals in the *Worker's Spokesman*.

Back inside the church the service was drawing to a close, and the paunched and balding preacher in his purple robes had already successfully stage-managed the exchanging of the rings and the signing of the book. He mopped his glistening brow with a loud handkerchief and pushed it manfully back into his pocket. Leila watched as a fly buzzed around his ears. For a moment the spell was broken as his eyes rolled aimlessly around his head. Then, as if nothing happened, the fly swerved away, bored and fatigued, and the magic returned. Straightening up, one hand pulling at his lapel, the preacher's voice boomed out: 'At this moment I would like to call upon the congregation to be upstanding.'

The preacher made a large skyward gesture with both arms. Then, throwing back his bull-like head, he endeavoured to take on the appearance of a man who was in constant contact with God, not just a casual acquaintance, but an intimate and life-long friend of the Holy Spirit himself.

49

'And now I would ask you to join together and sing with me hymn number 47.'

Leila stood before him, feeling like a spectator at her own wedding. Then the organ burst forth and the preacher began to bellow out the words to an unfamiliar hymn, a hymn which curved upwards in search of an understanding heaven.

The church hall was cluttered with neither pew nor altar, idol nor performer. Around its perimeter there lay, neatly arranged in a correct rectangle, the tables which laboured under the burden of the food and drink. Plums, mangoes, sugar cakes, rice and meat, pears, ginger beer, soursop, lemonade, rum; the tables were laid as if for a country feast. At the end of the hall the double doors were thrown wide open, allowing a fresh breeze to circulate and the sweet smell of the food and drink to sting the afternoon air. Immediately outside the door the wispy grass swept down towards the trees of a cool coconut grove where the land was even grassier. From there, like tall thin legs, the trees marched without discipline towards the placid turquoise sea. Beyond the sea the soft gentle peaks of the smaller sister island, today light green and definite in their outline, sulked on the horizon.

The open doors allowed guests to slip outside into the sun and talk there if they wanted to, before coming back in for more food and drink. Some did so but, at least to start with, most stayed inside.

Leila, her body small and hot beneath her gown, felt assailed on all sides by well-wishers and those who just wanted to feel the cloth. She kept mixing up false smiles with real ones, 'I'm very happy's' with 'Thank you for coming's', the kissing of some people on the cheek with the shaking of other people's hands. Everybody was too polite to say anything when she got things wrong, and when they had finished they just stood back and gazed at her. Leila pretended not to notice the number of eyes on her, but inside she panicked, feeling that maybe her white bridal gown was really black to their eyes, or else something was hanging from her hair, or an earring was about to fall out. But she was not able to examine herself, knowing that once she started she would merely descend into a paroxysm of twitching and scratching, checking and double checking, so she stood transfixed as her temperature rose by the minute, easily outstripping the temperature of the air in the hall.

Michael and Bradeth were the last to escape the sun's heat and take refuge inside the hall. They had discarded their jackets and ties long before going outside, and they now stood just inside the doors, jackets thrown over their shoulders and ties tucked out of sight in their trouser pockets. They looked back down the slope towards the sea.

'So you make she pregnant, then?' Michael spilled his drink as he spoke. He was clearly drunk.

'Hush nuh, man. You want everyone to hear you?'

'It's a secret, then? A big secret?' asked Michael.

'Sure it's a secret. I don't want everyone to hear, you know.'

'But look, man, they going find out sometime, or you planning on giving she a gin bath?' laughed Michael.

'I not planning on giving she anything.'

'Well, not anything more than what you did already give to she.'

Michael laughed too loudly at his own joke, but Bradeth was unmoved. He stood quietly, his eyes wide and inviting, like the petite saucers of some delicate tea service, eyes which together with his trousers which had mischievously crept up high above his red woollen socks, gave him the appearance of being an alert and intelligent boy who had outgrown his school uniform.

'Why you not take up some protection?' asked Michael.

Bradeth laughed incredulously. 'You telling me about protection? Who it is used to give the girls Phensic telling them it's contraceptive pill?'

'If it make them feel better then nothing wrong with giving them a pill of some kind. Anyhow, it always work out alright.'

'Always?' asked Bradeth.

51

Michael paused for a moment before replying. 'Well, Beverley don't be the type of woman you can just fool like that, and beside it don't matter with she.'

Bradeth sucked his teeth. He dabbed at his brow with a freshly laundered handkerchief. Michael swilled the rum punch around in his glass, took a drink and swallowed.

The reception was losing some of its excitement in the energy-sapping heat, and everybody now seemed to be anxiously seeking refuge as part of a group. They chattered away, seemingly frightened to detach themselves in case they could not find a point of entry into another group. The few lonely exceptions seemed bored, but somehow comfortable in their boredom, like sentries on duty. To the centre of the hall the preacher was talking with a beaming Millie, but as far as Michael was concerned, Bradeth apart, there was nobody to talk to and nothing to talk about. He turned and looked out of the double doors again. Then he drifted away down the slope towards the sea. Bradeth shrugged his shoulders and followed.

'Bradeth, tell me what colour you think your child going come? White, fusty, musty, dusty, tea, coffee, cocoa, light black, black or dark black? You remember that saying?'

'Don't be an arse. Sure I remember the saying,' snapped Bradeth.

'And what about the child hair and complexion? Fair skin, good hair, rough skin, kinky hair, ringlets, or maybe it's a mulatto child you going get?'

Bradeth's patience was expiring. 'What the fuck you talking about, man?'

'I talking about the child,' said Michael, 'the child you give she to have.'

Bradeth looked away, his skin bristling with anger, but he could feel Michael's eyes burning into him. There was a brief pause, then Michael spoke again.

'You see these people,' he said, gesturing up the hill, 'and how much food they be eating off, and all the drink they be drinking.'

Bradeth did not reply.

'You know,' said Michael, seemingly oblivious to Bradeth's wrath, 'If I has a son I just going give him a ten dollars and tell him go fuck off to some other island to get married, for I sure I can't afford all of this nonsense. Or even better still I tell him not to bother at all, for why a man should buy cow if he can get milk free?'

Bradeth turned to face him, his damp face catching the sunlight, his small head shaved so close that it seemed a shame not to take off all the hair.

'Look, man, why you not go see to your wife?' Bradeth spoke slowly, his words spiked with indignation. 'I sure she going appreciate a bit of affection on she wedding day.' Michael laughed alone and spilled more drink.

'Let me tell you, man, you might have the common sense not to marry to the woman just for you put she with child, but still it's me who you learn that lesson from. Now a next lesson you must learn is how to keep a wife in she place after you done take one up so why you don't just lock off your mouth and observe me over the next few days, for I know when it's affection time and when it's coolness time.'

'What it is you trying to do?' asked Bradeth, elbows adrift as he wiped off the perspiration from underneath his collar. For a moment Michael lost his balance and he grabbed at Bradeth's arm and pulled himself upright.

'I don't be trying to do nothing, man. There's nothing here for me to do, nothing!' Michael gestured wildly. 'Nothing, man!'

With that he walked away from Bradeth, up the hill and back into the hall. He saw Millie talking with the preacher and he jostled his way across to her.

'Where Leila be?' asked Michael. The preacher stopped talking and Millie pointed coldly to a door which led off from the hall.

In the corner Leila sat crying, her face buried in her hands, her body hunched. As she heard the door close she looked up at Michael both relieved and ashamed to see him. She tried to stop the tears. Her white bridal gown looked spotless, all the more so in a room as gloomy as this one. Then she unbent herself and smiled, her creased brow betraying her true anxiety.

'So what you crying for?' asked Michael. More drink slopped from his glass. 'And what you doing hiding away in here like you is escaped convict or something?' Michael had a habit of pointing with his little finger when he got angry. He stabbed vigorously at the air, poking holes into space.

'Nothing,' whispered Leila.

'What you mean, nothing? Nothing is nothing. There has to be a reason. You not want to tell it me?'

Leila looked up at her husband and then away from him again. She opened her mouth to speak but inevitably she stuttered badly.

'It's just that I was going to ask you if it was time to cut the cake and my mother said it was but you should have the decency not to drink so much that you would completely forget all the details of your own wedding day.' She paused, but Michael's face registered no emotion. 'Do you love me, Michael? The least you can do is tell me that.'

'Tell you what? You sitting in here crying over some fucking wedding cake instead of being out there with all your friends and family.'

Leila stared at him, but Michael continued, 'As if fucking wedding cake is important issue on a day like this.' Michael steadied himself and strengthened his tone. 'I tell you what is important issue, me!' he said, knocking hand and glass into his chest, 'or maybe you don't think so?'

'Of course I think you're important.'

Michael threw the rest of his drink in her face and turned to go, but as he reached the door Leila's crippled mother stood before him. For a brief moment they stopped and faced each other in the doorway, then he swept past her into the loud, brightly coloured, happy church hall, and he charged through the double doors and down the hill towards the sea.

Her mother looked lamely at her daughter. She shut the door behind her, blocking out both the noise and the light. From her sleeve she pulled clear a white lace handkerchief. Without meeting her child's eyes, she pressed it into Leila's warm hand. Then she left the reception hall and made her way home.

Leila pulled the handkerchief from her dampened grip and wiped her face. Never before had her mother left her, but though she felt deserted she knew she had already cried too much. She got up, found a mirror on the wall and looked hard at herself. A wife and a woman. A woman and a wife. She shut her teeth tight with frustration, knowing she would go out there and talk to her husband as if nothing had happened. That was the way it would have to be. Later, when he had forgotten, she would mention it again just to let him know that she had not forgotten.

Michael walked along the beach and listened. To his right the sea murmured and gently swelled, with only the occasional white fleck spoiling the view. Though the flecks were small they looked to Michael grossly out of place, like spots of toothpaste on a bathroom mirror. He turned away and began automatically to increase his pace. He knew where he was going, but before he got there he wanted to think. His body, blindly following his mind, began to race, and his feet strayed carelessly into the dying surf.

By the time he arrived at Beverley's house she had already put their son to bed behind the curtain. She crossed the room and took Michael's dinner from the rough oven. As she did so she picked up a bottle of beer for him to drink with it. Then she sat by the front door and watched the moon appear. Michael looked at her back. She seemed to be able to understand things without his having to explain. At least there was that. But she

55

was too placid, just nothing. He stabbed at his food and drank a hasty mouthful of beer.

In the twilight Leila sat on her mother's step, resting up her back against the shuttered house. Stretched out in front of her a lengthy shadow, her own, lay sullen against the grainy street. In the distance she watched Bradeth and Millie fade away, two shapes, one long, one short, arms locked around each other. They were making their way back down towards town having accompanied Leila up to St Patrick's in Mr Johnson's taxi. Mr Johnson was now going on round the island at his own pace, so the two of them had decided to walk back and try and pick up a lift on the way. Leila watched them, knowing they would spend the night at Bradeth's place making love till early morning, but she did not want to think about this. As the night put out the day her thoughts drifted back to the church hall.

She had stayed until the end of the reception. Apart from the preacher, she and Bradeth and Millie had been the last to leave. The preacher, looking even more obese without his purple robes, drew a hand down his face and left behind a smile.

'Where Michael is, or should I say your husband?' His face split like a coconut and his teeth poured out. 'He leave you already?'

In one movement Leila pushed back her mop of black hair and wiped the light perspiration from her brow with her mother's lace handkerchief.

'You land a good man there, for he got something about him that most the other boys on this island just don't got, so mind you look after him well.'

Millie shuffled her feet nervously, and the preacher began to giggle like an aged clown.

'And I sure whatever it is he got you going find out about it tonight!' He leaned back, closed his drunken eyes and roared with laughter.

Outside Mr Johnson was leaning up against the side of his

taxi waiting for her. He had brought Leila to her wedding and on to the reception, and he would take her home. But as they drove off, Bradeth and Millie having joined them, nobody spoke.

Leila got up from the doorstep and went inside the house. As she slipped quickly out of her bridal gown she could hear her mother's quiet coughing and she stood and listened. Her mother coughed with the same low noise that the wind made as it brushed through the trees. The occasional squeal of the bed was the only other sound that came from her mother's room.

Having taken off the gown, Leila could smell the sweet scent of the day's perspiration which had settled dew-like on the parts of her skin that had been tightly covered up. She walked back into the front room, filled a small tin bath half-full with cold water and washed her body, taking care not to splash too much water out on to the floor. Then she wrapped a long towel around her shoulders and dripped her way across the room. She stopped at the small wooden table and ran her damp finger down the dusty spine of the still spread-eagled book. Leila wondered if she would ever finish reading the book to her mother. She walked back into her bedroom and closed the door before peeling off the towel and standing naked. The drops of water on her body turned cold and she began to shiver. She had already admitted to herself that he would not come so she climbed into bed, sneezed and turned over.

The next morning the murderous cry of the crowing cock woke Leila with a start. Her first night as a married woman had passed by without incident. She lay in bed and listened to her mother who was getting up. Leila dared not imagine what she must be thinking of her. But, as she heard her beginning to boil some water, Leila again drifted off into a light sleep, though the dull and obedient sounds of a new day provided for her the background noises which would ensure her restlessness.

Again Leila woke up with a start. She listened, but this time she heard nothing, so she presumed her mother asleep. She lay in bed like a waxen dummy, her shock of hair a deeper black against the white pillow and forming a nest-like down on which to rest her head. She had dreamed but she could not remember what it was she had dreamed about. If it had been a bad dream she would have remembered, and the same would have been true if it had been a particularly good dream. It was just nothing, but then again the pillow was wet. She turned it over and decided there was little point in her getting up.

Throughout the day she tossed and turned. She thought about things she did not really want to think about, but things she could not banish from her mind. Eventually the day ran its true course and Leila slipped away into a deep, wearisome sleep. She awoke just once to hear her mother coughing and spitting at the darkest point of the night, but she fell asleep again, unsure as to how to offer any help. As she slept she dreamed again, but this time she would re-member her dream for it would be more than fiction, a memory as opposed to an invention.

Another hour had drifted by. Millie picked up a smooth stone and tossed it gently down the hill. It bounced a few times then began to roll, at first quickly, then slowly, finally coming to a halt long before the bottom of the slope. Millie stood up, her small body blocking the sun's light from Leila's face.

'Move, Millie,' said Leila, squinting at her friend's back, her head resting in her cupped palms. 'Do you want me to sit in the dark?'

Millie sucked her teeth. 'I don't want you risk getting a tan,' she said, without bothering to turn around. Then she moved off to the right, letting the light flood back into Leila's face. Leila quickly shielded her eyes with both hands. She knew now that something was the matter, for Millie was acting like a sullen child, something she was seldom prone to do despite the fact that she looked like one.

It was Millie who had insisted that they come and sit halfway up the hill among the nettles and long razor grass and have a talk, but that was some hours ago now. To begin with Millie had sat by Leila and looked out to sea, saying nothing. Leila had assumed that she just wanted to take in the view of the island, which from this height unfolded before them like a fully blossomed flower, then wander back down to the village. But then Millie had stood up without saying anything. Then she had sat down again. Now she was standing. Leila said nothing. What it was Millie was playing at, what it was she actually had on her mind, Leila was unsure, but she felt it might be to do with Michael who she knew (nobody had told her, she just knew) would soon ask her to marry him.

Millie bent and picked a piece of grass. She tore it apart as if her life depended upon it. In the far distance a small fishing boat (a charred splinter floating in the sea) drifted towards the island, slowly, as if laden down with fish, but it was probably empty and slow simply because there was nothing to hurry back for. They both looked. Up above the sky was clear and not even the merest rag of a cloud swirled into view. Out on the horizon, beyond the boat, where sky met sea, the world split in two, the lower half made up of metallic silver, the upper half of some softly spun, precious blue cloth.

Millie turned around, alarmed, her mouth half-opened as if the words would never come. She swallowed lumpily, then seized the moment.

'But Leila, the man already done put one woman with child and I sure he don't tell you it's so he do, so I telling you.' Again she swallowed. 'He tell you?'

Leila dropped her eyes and fidgeted.

'I know about the woman and the child. It's just his way.'

'What you mean is just his way? He think you is a dog or what? He think she is a dog? He think he can just go put whatever woman with child he feel like and then go walk out with a next one like nothing is the matter, or he be a saint or something?'

'But he's told me about her and how it is she feels and all the rest of it.'

'You think she don't be nothing because her man done leave she?'

'What are you talking about, Millie?'

'You think like man now, you think she just be something he can go mess around with when he do feel like it?'

'I don't know what you're talking about!'

'I don't know why you do lie to me so, Leila, I don't know why, for the only thing wrong with you, and it's going get you in trouble, is the fact that you is a coward, you too damn scared to come out and admit when you done something wrong or when you do make a mistake.' Millie paused, lips pursed, then went on, 'I know for true that Michael don't tell you nothing about she for Bradeth say he always joking to him about what he do say to woman and what he don't say, and how it's up to woman to figure this out and to figure that out, so why you can't be real with me, Leila, why you can't just say to me the man don't tell you as yet and that's all there be to it, why you can't say that?'

'I can.'

'Well, say it then, be honest with me, don't pretend, don't be a coward with me if I'm really your best friend, don't pretend to me, alright! Don't pretend to me!'

Millie spun around and ran back down the hill. Soon she disappeared from view. Then Leila looked up and watched the sun begin its long slide into the sea. Michael had not told her. She had lied. But she knew about the child for it was easy to find out these things, even if you did not want to find them out. In fact she knew even before Arthur left that this man who had been paying so much attention to her had been harbouring a pregnant woman, a woman who now had a child, but she felt that the woman was a nothing woman to him and it did not worry her. He did not even mention her. Maybe she should have said this to Millie. But then she might have looked a fool and angered Millie even more. She lay back, hands behind her head, and thought of Michael.

It was only a few months ago that he had roared into St Patrick's, hugging the tight curve with the bike like a child tracing a circle with a pencil. Leila heard the low buzz of the horn, but she continued to squeeze the lemon into the glass jug. A pip squirted out and scuttled across the floor. Leila crossed the room, bent over and picked it up. As she straightened up the horn sounded out again and this time she went to the door to look.

Michael sat casually on the bike, one foot resting flat against the ground, the other tucked up into the belly of the machinery. It was late afternoon and the sun caught the chrome and reflected short, intense shafts of light, scattering them in all directions. A large cloud of dust tumbled down the street. Michael did not move, neither did he turn his head or lift up his hand to protect his eyes. It passed by, leaving Michael a little dustier but the image intact.

'Come, I going take you for a ride, so put down your things and let we go, nuh.'

Leila pivoted slightly, wondering whether she should tell her mother, but she thought otherwise. If she was awake then she would have heard anyhow. Leila dashed inside, put the stray pip on the table and wiped her hands on a cloth. She rushed out as she was.

Leila had never been on a bike and the sensation shocked her. It was the freedom which struck her most, the idea that for a brief moment you could escape behind a wall of sound and speed, unsure as to whether you would ever emerge from it. As the cane and trees and shrub went spinning past she clung tightly to Michael, playfully digging her fingers into his firm flesh.

'Where we going?' she shouted. 'Where you taking me?'

'Black Rocks,' bellowed Michael. 'Black Rocks! We can just ease off and talk when we get there.'

The wind lifted his voice from her ears but she heard most of his words. It was all part of the thrill. She tightened her arms around Michael in a warm human belt.

He parked the bike and lay down in the late afternoon sun. Leila climbed off and lay next to him. She looked up and breathed deeply and regularly. But by the time she had relaxed from the ride and was ready to reach over and touch Michael, he had fallen asleep.

Leila looked at his face and began to worry. In the rush of it all she had not noticed how tired he looked. She had never before seen him asleep, and his face looked like a bridge that had collapsed into a pile of rubble. Beneath his eyelids his eyes still darted left and right, and his lips kept parting, quietly at first, then with more vigour as he begun to mutter to himself. As she rolled over on to her back Leila realized he had not yet explained about the bike, or why he wanted to bring her here. In fact he had not explained about anything. For a moment she thought about waking him up but she knew it was unfair. In reality Leila was convinced that Beverley must have bought the bike for him. The sea continued to smash into the Black Rocks and Michael continued to sleep; Leila's thoughts became twisted and difficult. She did not know the woman. She had seen her close-up, just once, but she had never spoken with her.

It had been a Monday, the slow traffic of the capital had begun to tire, the school buses had been and gone and even the stealthy cars seemed to have ground to a halt. Only the odd bicycle flew past, its furious master inevitably young, barechested and vociferous. The only other activity in Baytown was in the open gutters where the waste ran smooth and yellow like melted butter. Leila kicked lazily at the road and watched the granular spray fly in all directions. As it was a warm afternoon she had decided to walk back some of the way home rather than catch a country bus.

She ambled along the straight road that led out of the capital toward St Patrick's. Then she saw Beverley holding her newborn child like a bundle of rags. She was standing as if waiting for a lift of some kind. To Leila it seemed more likely that drivers would stop to ask after her sanity, rather than her destination, for she stood with her head uncovered. Leila panicked, realizing that she was nearly on top of the woman. She did not know what to do and it was clearly too late for her to turn around or to go back. She pressed on, her heart thumping heavily.

Beverley, small and plump, her face freckled, her breasts large, milk-filled, turned to look at Leila as she passed her by. She stared at her as a native stares at a tourist, and Leila pretended she did not realize she was being mocked by somebody's silent eyes. She tried desperately not to quicken her pace or change her posture. She just walked and walked and walked, suddenly feeling the full fire of the sun. The baby's face was all she had managed to see and it looked like Michael. The same deep colour, the same eyes that said nothing, the mouth, everything.

Once out of sight Leila stopped and felt the perspiration gushing down her face. The baby was still haunting her and she took a deep breath. She wiped her face on a handkerchief and dabbed at her nose. Then she began to move off again, this time at a quicker pace, then she slowed, realizing she did not even know the name of Michael's child, and there was nobody she could ask.

The second day followed the same depressing pattern. Leila woke, lay in bed, thought and listened. She had dreamed, and she had little difficulty in remembering what it was she had dreamed about. As she listened, only the voices from the street disturbed the silence of the house. Her mother did not get out of bed. For Leila the birds stopped singing at the right time, and the sun burned its predictable way down towards the next night, and again she was tired.

Night fell and dampened the noises in the street. Only the occasional human voice dared compete with the shrieking insects. Man's interest in the day was coming to an end. Inside Leila's room the shadows were still, and after two days the air heavy and making her want to cough; but she held back, not wanting to wake her mother. She swallowed deeply, then, waiting until she heard her mother's irregular breathing attain some semblance of normality, she threw back the sheet and crept out of bed. She dressed quickly, passed out of the bedroom into the neglected front room, and from there into the moonlight.

Michael's wedding present lay against the side of the house. Leila was unsure if she would be able to push it, but she would try. She peeled back the noisy tarpaulin covering, knocked the stand away and struggled to keep it upright. The moon caught its long silver tubing. Leila was sure that as long as she could keep it balanced she would manage. She lowered her head, dropped her shoulders, leaned forward and began pushing with large strides.

The road was empty and dead. Even the fine dust beneath her feet and the dust beneath the reluctant wheels remained undisturbed. To her right a cool breeze blew in off the sea, whose whisperings she could hear, though she knew not what was being said. She pushed on, her slender arms growing quickly numb. Then the moon unwrapped itself from a cloud, the night softened a little and Leila paused to catch her breath. Then she pressed on again.

Off to her left and trapped in a mesh of cane, Leila saw the rusting bulk of an overturned car. It made her feel uneasy. She began to think aimlessly, and her mind blundered upon her father, and her head turned slightly as if avoiding derisive eyes. It was his money that had bought the bike, and though Leila had always presumed him dead there was no reason for this to be so. The money that was paid to her mother might be from his will, or from the revenue of his estate, if he had an estate. She had always thought that he must have one, but then again perhaps he paid the money in himself. Perhaps he was still alive? Leila stopped and listened to the insects, knowing that she had to empty her mind of these thoughts for they embarrassed her now as they had always done in the past. 'Mulatto girl,' 'Mulatto girl,' was what her friends at school used to sing at her, and Leila used to run away and hide and wish that her mother would tell her it was not true. But her mother never said anything, and Leila used to look at her and wonder if her mother had ever been in love with her father, whoever he was.

Leila arrived and pulled back the bike on to its stand. She looked up at the crooked outline of the building. From Beverley's house there came no noise. The simple frame cast a deep shadow. She felt her skirt sticking to her legs, and for an instant she thought the bike must have leaked some petrol. She reached down and realized that it was just more perspiration. Leila prepared herself to walk back the 6 miles she had just come, knowing if she was going to get there before dawn she would have to forget her tiredness and start walking now. Then, from inside the house, a baby screamed and Leila's heart tumbled down a flight of stairs and she ran.

She arrived exhausted but relieved in front of her mother's house. In the warmth of a clear Caribbean dawn, the sea and sky were once again a life-supporting blue. But she did not linger to look. Leila went through into her room, took off her clothes and slid into bed as the cock crowed for the last time.

She was awoken by the sound of a motorbike, and from the light she could see that it was now late afternoon. Michael announced his arrival by roaring the engine of his new bike, then skidding it to an exaggerated halt. He climbed down, dusted off his clean clothes, then adjusted his royal blue tie. He folded his hand in readiness to knock lightly on the door, but Leila had already crawled out of bed and rushed to open it. She stood before him and flinched when she saw his raised fist.

Seeing her reaction, Michael lowered his hand and looked at his wife. 'You just get up?'

Leila nodded and pulled her dressing gown close.

'And it's you who bring down the bike?' She nodded again.

'The old one only good for spare parts now,' said Michael.

They stood and stared at each other, then Michael shuffled his feet and spoke clumsily.

'Well, it's no wonder you tired, then. Maybe I should go and let you have some peace and quiet.'

He made a slight move to leave but she was quick to catch him, her own words equally clumsy.

'No, come in.'

She stepped back and to the side, and Michael slipped past her and sat down at the table. Leila left the door open and moved over to pour him some ginger beer from a tall glass jug. She set both glass and jug before him, and as she pulled back her hand he grabbed at it. They looked at each other. Then Michael spoke.

'At the wedding. I was drunk and acting the fool.' He paused. 'I feel I ought to make a new start.'

Leila slipped away.

'You hungry?' she asked, lifting a heavy pot with her two thin arms.

'Yes,' said Michael.

Leila cooked him the food and he ate in silence. He pushed the plate away and again he looked at her.

'You want to help me make a new start or we done finish before we even really begin?'

Leila looked closely at him, his face clean shaven, the area around the upper lip having been shaved a little too close as the pores there seemed almost cavernous.

'I don't think we've finished before we've started,' she said. Michael leaned over and kissed her firstly on her cheeks, then on her slightly parted, already dampened lips. They were in their third day of married life.

Leila moved cautiously away from the table. She sat on the doorstep and began to soak up the sun. Michael joined her and for the rest of the afternoon they sat, talked and looked the part. Then, as their short day drew to a close, they got up and went through to Leila's bedroom.

*

Leila woke up alone and feeling sick. Her body had slept but her head had not had a moment's peace. Her face felt old and crumpled, like a once-read, now-discarded newspaper. Outside a cock began to crow, unsure of whether it wanted to go through with another day in this powerful heat. The days were lengthening and again the island was preparing itself for a small rebirth. It was that time of the year. It had already rained, and the mushlike vegetation had rotted and devoured itself, and the winds had blown, and the hurricane warnings had been sounded, and the crickets had screeched in fear, but there was nothing to fear.

The afternoons had begun to get hotter, the sun had blistered and the swollen clouds started to appear in the sky, initially just the one, later whole flocks of them. Then a gust of wind picked a dry leaf from a tree and sent it spinning to the ground, and in the distance, over the sea, a dark grey roof of cloud supported by vertical columns, their foundations in the heart of the ocean, brooded ominously. The rains were coming.

Then a great clap of thunder had cleaved the earth clean in half. The huge metal spike appeared in the sky for two, three seconds at a time and the first few lazy drops were released. A dry, low patter of rain, and everybody could pretend it was winter. Then came the blinding rain and the children ran crazily, getting heavier and heavier, until that one vast and final crack and flash shook their growing bodies and their limbs

67

began to move with a new freedom and ease. They danced round and round, arms thrown up, fingers outstretched, their faces streaming, and they were happy knowing they could not get any wetter.

Then later the whole sky became grey, and the dull incessant beat began to drain the spirit. The cars swished uncaringly by, and the bullets of rain no longer stung. The individual sounds began to distinguish themselves, the rain beating on leaves, on puddles, on grass, on rain itself. Over the hills the mist hung thick and bold, and the wind rushed into the trees which shook off their water only to be drowned again.

And then a light, almost breathless wind brushed aside the heavy clouds, leaving only drifting balls of feathery wool, too young to hold rain; and soon after God's hand fashioned the perfect arch of the rainbow.

And later the cane leaves turned brown, the earth grew dusty and the juice ripened through into the shorter days and cooler evenings of December and January. February was uneventful (it was not a leap year). Now it was March and the confident days were quick to seize the morning light, reluctant to give way to the peace of the evening. It was that time of the year.

After two weeks of relative stability Michael had again started to go around to Beverley's. Then, when Leila's pregnancy reached its middle stages, and her swollen shape no longer held any mystery, he started to spend nearly all his time with Beverley. These days Leila seldom saw him, but she tried to think of him even less. A few weeks ago he had called by to collect some clothes and she had let him in. He looked well and only his hair, usually short and wiry, seemed a little matted and out of place, but Michael would have no doubt already taken note of this. They said nothing, and he gathered up his clothes and left. That evening Leila sat angrily and cursed herself for not having had the nerve to have said something to him. But she could think of nothing that would have made any impression upon him. In fact he did not even seem to have noticed her.

The cock stopped crowing and Leila eased out from underneath the damp sheet and levered herself, and the child she carried, up off the side of the bed. She stood crooked, thinking it too much trouble to get dressed for she was not going anywhere. She pulled on a dressing gown, stepped into her slippers and moved slowly into the front room. Leila tried to be as quiet as possible, for hearing neither her mother's cracked breathing nor her sinister coughing, she presumed her asleep. But as she reached down for the beaten kettle she noticed the envelope. The name on the front was in her mother's spidery writing. Leila picked it up and moved as quickly as the child in her belly would allow her to. She opened her mother's bedroom door.

The bed had been stripped down and the linen sheets folded neatly at the foot of it. The caseless pillow sat at the head of the bed where it ought to be, and the room looked freshly dusted and cleaned. A tiny window had been propped open to allow the air to circulate, otherwise everything was still. It looked like what Leila had always imagined a cheap hotel would look like. Sterile and impersonal. Somebody had lived here once but they could not have been very happy. And they had left having made a decision. Leila tore at the letter, and the envelope circled its way to the floor.

'Dear daughter, I think you know where I have gone to and why it is I . . .'

Leila loosened her grip, then she tightened it again. Her eyes roamed over the words.

'The doctor has advised me that . . . If there is a God somewhere . . .'

By now she was gripping the letter so hard it was as if she was trying to squeeze the ink out of it. Her mother had left for England.

'He said either I die here or I go to where there is . . .'

Leila sat on the edge of the empty bed and let her foot brush against the envelope. She listened to the children congregating in the street before being sent off to school. She listened to their anxious mothers, to their impatient fathers, to their own hectic voices, and her mind hissed and she could tell she was skirting the edge of a deep depression, for England seemed so far away that she could not believe her mother would ever come back from such a place.

There was a knock at the door and Leila jumped. She waited a moment, but whoever it was had decided not to knock again. Leila left her mother's bedroom and made her way to the door. She saw Bradeth first, his long legs like two burnt matchsticks, and behind him stood Millie holding their baby girl, Shere. Millie spoke first, the morning light catching her face.

'Well, here I am.'

She came forward and delivered Shere into her godmother's arms with care and affection, almost ceremony, much as a child would offer a favourite doll to another child. Bradeth picked up the bags by his side and carried them into the room. He set them down lightly in the middle of the floor, then pulled up a chair and turned to Leila.

'Leila, take the weight off your feet, nuh.' He took his daughter, leaving Millie to guide Leila into the chair.

They smiled nervously, close friends acting like strangers. Then they were quiet. Millie broke the silence.

'Remember last week when I tell you that my Aunt Toosie don't like the idea of no unmarried woman and child round she shop?' Leila nodded. 'Well, since Shere born she practically stop talking to Bradeth, so maybe it's as well your mother gone to England and I can move in here. Save me breaking up with my aunt. I can also help with the baby when it come.'

'I see,' said Leila. 'I understand.'

They fell silent again, and the noises from the street died away as the children finally made their way to school. The atmosphere was wrong. Bradeth knew he should never have knocked on the door. He and Millie should have just walked in like they usually did, as if nothing was the matter. For a few moments he played with his daughter, then he looked up and saw that both Millie and Leila were watching him, seemingly absorbed in his every movement.

'I have to get to town now for I have a big order that I need Michael to deliver.'

He stopped there, realizing what he had just said. Millie's small face hardened and Bradeth caught her look. He would not say any more. Drawing himself to his full height, he garbled a final sentence. 'I better go now before I miss the bus back to town. I going drop in on you both tomorrow.'

He kissed his daughter and passed her to Millie. Then he pressed his lips against Millie's forehead, smiled at Leila and disappeared briskly through the open door.

Millie passed Shere across to Leila. She stood and poured her a glass of coconut water, then she poured one for herself and sat back down. It was not yet nine in the morning. Leila began to cry. Millie leaned over to take Shere, but Leila held on. Millie put down her glass, knelt and slipped her short arm around Leila's shoulder.

'What is it?' asked Millie, but Leila cried without moving a muscle, as if out of consideration for the child on her lap.

'You can't tell me what it is?' Leila's trickle of tears became a stream and she could not talk. 'Don't worry,' Millie reassured her. 'There's two of us now and we'll both get by. We'll manage.'

But Leila sat with a vague and detached gaze, her mouth like a jagged cut.

*

The following week Leila gave birth. It was early evening. The shadows of the sloping trees had begun their stretching across the road, and the sister wood in the houses creaked and snapped, cooled down and joined in the long wait for the moon. The unbridled wind cantered down the road, turning bits of litter, creeping in every backyard, rustling every leaf. In one hundred darkened rooms one hundred darkened hands reached out and turned up their kerosene lamps, knowing full well that night would soon fall and a naked flame would be their sun-substitute till the morning.

Inside the house Millie held a pan of hot water with both hands. She looked on helplessly as Leila, horizontal, legs hitched and parted, as if someone had thrown open a pair of light brown double doors, strained mercilessly. In the background a fan buzzed, but it merely turned over the heavy air and it settled again. Bradeth, feeling awkward and out of place, stood back and tried to find more shadow. A lone cricket cried out. Overtures and beginners.

The white nurse, sweat pouring from her spinster's brow, encouraged the young girl. 'Just once more, Leila.' She paused. 'That's it, just once more, dear.' The nurse talked with anxious concentration.

In the fading light Leila twisted and tried to force the unborn child from her body. One hand was folded, redundant, behind her head, the other clung to the metal frame on the side of the bed.

'Just once more, Leila, just once more, dear.'

Millie hovered, water in pan, wishing the pain would leave her friend's body. Then the nurse took the pan of hot water from her. Millie, physically unburdened, crossed her fingers and continued to urge Leila on, her own small frame eager to share some of the pain. Then, as if it were the most natural thing in the world, Leila began to moan, at first softly, then louder, as the child began to ease its bloody way out from between her legs.

'Nearly there now. Nearly there,' said the nurse.

Leila, her lips bunched, her forehead knotted, snatched for

breath and lay back even further, pushing her body down into the mattress as if she wanted to disappear from sight.

The nurse lifted the crying boy clear of Leila's body and she wiped his skin. Millie uncrossed her fingers and came forward.

'You alright?'

Leila did not open her eyes, she just nodded.

'Sure?' asked Millie again, her mouth hanging loose.

Leila opened her eyes. 'I'm sure.'

The nurse spoke with well-practised awe. 'It's a boy. A healthy-looking boy of about eight pounds.'

Leila's hands stretched forward to take the child, and the nurse willingly gave him to her. Then, with almost automatic ease, the nurse began to take off her apron and collect her utensils. For her the day was at an end.

Millie pushed back the child's shiny black hair.

'The child dark like Shere. Much darker than you.'

Leila looked her son in the face, his cheeks gleaming like small lumps of black coal. 'I know,' she said. 'I can see that.'

His eyes were tightly shut and his miniature hands fastened close as if ready for battle. Like his mother's his upper lip was split but his lower lip was slightly swollen, as though someone had already hit him. Leila peeled back his pocket-sized shawl and looked for signs of any marks on his body. There were none. He was clean and still and brown and he had finished his crying.

Bradeth stood in his closely guarded shadow, having shown no emotion throughout the whole process. He had not been present when his own daughter was born, for Shere's had been a premature birth. When it became clear that Leila was almost certain to give birth this evening he did not return to the capital as he had planned. He followed Millie's instructions, borrowed a bicycle and cycled into Sandy Bay for the nurse. Then he had cycled back up the road with her as furiously as he could.

It was almost dark now and Millie played with the newborn child, gently rubbing her girl's finger up against his tiny nose. The nurse had packed her bags and she stood ready to leave. She spoke to Millie. 'I'll leave you to it then, if I may.'

Millie turned to face her, but the nurse looked past her. 'And I'll drop by and see you tomorrow, Mrs Preston.'

The nurse hardly waited for an answer. She crossed the bedroom and managed not to see Bradeth. Then she moved into the front room and out into the warm evening air. They all listened as she mounted her bicycle and began to pedal her way back down the island towards Sandy Bay.

Leila finished listening and closed her eyes. Millie slipped away to where Bradeth was standing and she looked up at him. 'You know where Michael is?' She spoke in a whisper.

'Sandy Bay someplace.'

'He should be here to give her some help and support.'

Bradeth looked across at Leila. Millie went on, 'The girl nearly sick with worry about her mother and now she have a child to think about and no man around the house.'

Bradeth nodded and shifted uneasily. 'I going talk to him. I don't know what it is he thinks he's playing at.'

Millie looked quizzically at Bradeth, surprised by the bitterness in his voice.

'I'll be here with Leila,' she said. 'I'll see you tomorrow.'

Bradeth squeezed her arm. 'You can manage till then?'

Millie nodded and he let go. He backed slowly out of the bedroom, for he knew the longer he stayed the more angry he would feel.

Bradeth climbed on the borrowed pushbike, knowing it would not take him long to cycle to Sandy Bay. He decided not to rush as there was nothing to rush for. He wanted to think. The winding road straightened out, now defined by the familiar wall of cane to his left, the hush of the sea to his right. Up ahead he saw the outline of the nurse, so he slowed down. He would not risk a conversation.

Though Bradeth was too big for most bicycles they eventually got him to where he wanted to go, despite the swerves and jolts he hated having to endure. He extended his legs like long tired pistons and gritted his teeth as the wheels crunched over small objects in the road, bits of cane, stones and old boxes. The breeze beat fiercely into his face and he slitted his eyes. Then, as he looked up ahead, he saw the nurse had pedalled out of sight, so he pushed on.

As he approached Michael's grandmother's house he braked gently. A lamp burned in the window, and trailing his sandalled foot in the dusty road, Bradeth slowed to a halt. He did not bother to dismount.

'Michael! You home, man?'

He waited, but his words hung eerily and unanswered in the night air. He shouted again, this time with greater anxiety.

'Michael! You home or what?'

But nobody answered and Bradeth made ready to swing the bicycle around. However, before he could raise one foot to the pedal, he heard the crackly voice he recognized as that of Michael's grandmother. It was as if the house was speaking back to him.

'I don't see Michael for some time now. He must be up by his wife in St Patrick's.'

Clearly Michael's grandmother did not recognize Bradeth's voice or she would have said something to him. Bradeth threw back a 'thank you' and cycled away.

When he reached Beverley's house Bradeth got off the bicycle and leaned it against the fence at the back. He looked over into the yard that was always swept spotlessly clean despite its poverty. Hens, goats, fruit trees, a tank for catching water; only the paling fence needed a few repairs doing to it, but he could not imagine Michael ever volunteering to do them.

Inside Michael sat by the lamplight, picking at his food with a clumsy fork. Beverley and Ivor sat in a corner. Beverley stared at nothing, but the child, now just over a year old, stared at its father, his small lips flapping open, unchecked by his mother's hand, pink on the inside.

There was a light knocking at the door. It dissipated, rather than created, tension. Without moving a muscle Beverley whispered admittance. 'Yes.'

Bradeth stepped from the darkness into the room. He did not shut the door behind him, preferring to hover, like a man who has just realized that he might possibly be an unwelcome guest. Michael glanced up at him, his face empty, then he went on playing with his food. Bradeth looked around. He had never before spoken with Beverley but they both knew well enough who the other was, and how they each fitted into Michael's life.

'I'm sorry to disturb you,' he said nervously.

Beverley let a smile run across her freckled face, then she looked down and cradled her son who stuck his thumb shyly into his mouth. Bradeth turned back towards Michael.

'I've come to have a word with you about something.'

Michael played for a few seconds, then let the fork drop down on to the plate. He pushed it away.

'Talk, then.'

He did not look up to face his friend, preferring to show him the top of his bowed head. Beverley gathered up her child and moved towards the curtain. Michael heard her move.

'Sit down!'

He had a knife in his voice. Beverley hesitated, then sat back down. Still standing, and feeling like a mast without a ship, Bradeth went on. He could feel his heart thumping faster and faster like an unrepentant fist in his chest.

'But I want to have a private word with you.'

Michael lifted his elbows off the table and slowly raised his head. He looked Bradeth straight in the face.

'Anything you have to say to me you say to she too, you hear me?'

'Well, then,' said Bradeth, 'Leila just born you a next son.'

There was a long pause.

'I said you have a next son. Your wife just give birth to a child.'

Bradeth stared at Michael. He was unable to look at Beverley for he felt ashamed of what his friend was forcing him to do.

Michael laughed. 'My arse,' he said, as if he had just been told a joke. 'Come, let we go for a drink and celebrate.' He pushed the chair back from the table and stood up.

Bradeth looked at him. 'What you say?'

'I said, come, let we go for a drink to celebrate the child's birth. You say it's a boy child?'

In his mind Bradeth saw the newborn child's face. He saw Leila's pain, and he forced himself to look at Beverley holding on to her son in the corner, seemingly unaware of what was going on. He looked back at Michael and for a moment he felt he wanted to punch him. But Bradeth's courage betrayed him. He turned and left. Michael sat back down and listened to the rattling of Bradeth's directionless pushbike. Then it was quiet again.

*

The night her son was born Leila did not sleep. The night after she managed only a few minutes, and the night after that a few minutes more. Despite her fatigue she had forgotten how to sleep. She would have to learn again, with Millie's help, though the noise of her son (whom she called Calvin) and Millie's daughter, Shere, only served to make this more difficult. However, as the weeks went by life became easier, and Leila began to sleep soundly. They were learning to live with each other as friends, as women, as mothers.

Another dawn seeped into Leila's room. It squeezed its way underneath the door and crept through the thin gap between the fluttering curtains. A weak ray crossed Calvin's face, his low-lying cot resting beside the bed. The same ray touched Arthur's unopened letter. Leila, awake but still numb with sleep, listened hard. She could hear no noise in the house though outside she heard the dead sound of a ripe fruit falling from a tree.

She pulled at the sheet and Arthur's letter slipped neatly and unnoticed off the side of the bed. Then she rolled from one side of the mattress to the next, trying to find a comfortable position, either on the pillow or off it. But she could not get back to sleep. She listened again, and this time in her mind she heard her mother's voice. Her muscles tightened with fear.

'So Arthur know anything about the boy from Sandy Bay?'

Leila lied. 'I've told him about Michael.'

'And you tell him it's this Michael boy walking you out now and he mustn't expect to come back from America and find you waiting for him?'

'I told him,' said Leila. 'And he understood.' She paused as her mother pursed her lips in disapproval, then rubbed at her headscarf.

'He understood,' she said, mimicking her daughter's voice. 'I take it you're happy with that?' Leila dropped her eyes and shook her head.

'I see, so you're not happy with that?' Leila waited as long as she dared, then looked up. 'I still like Arthur but two years is a long time and Michael . . .'

Her mother cut her short, her voice sharp. 'I suppose to you two years must seem like a long time, but you can take it from me that two years is no time at all. No time.'

Leila cleared her throat and tried to sound positive. 'It wouldn't matter if it were ten years,' she said. She spoke too abruptly. The rest of her words dried up. It was her mother who spoke first, and this time she did so quietly. 'It probably wouldn't, would it? Two years, ten years, ten minutes, you done make up your choice and I suppose you just going to have to live with it.'

Leila looked away but her mother continued, 'You better get to your bed now.'

Leila stood, leaned forward and kissed her mother lightly on the cheek, but her mother's skin felt unresponsive and cold with disappointment.

Earlier that evening Leila had kissed Arthur softly on the cheek and he too had felt cold, but it was more the sea breeze than a decline in mood that had cooled his skin. However, the staleness of his response still ached on her lips. They walked on and together they watched the sea throw out her weary branches, stutter and recede to momentary stillness. Above them they saw the brown and green palms become warm silhouettes. Then they sat, Arthur's arm draped casually like an old and trusted shawl around Leila's shoulders. With his loose hand Arthur lightly twisted her hair and she smiled. The sand beneath them still held the warmth of the day's heat, and a few yards to their left a deserted towel sulked on the darker sand, the sea lapping up against its feathered edges.

Arthur was a thin boy whose curly hair was clinically greased down, though the odd unruly curl spiralled away from the rest. His eyes were dark, his face narrow, and on his upper lip he had the shadowed outline of a thin moustache. His black-rimmed spectacles hung playfully on the end of his nose, so much so that he always appeared as if he was speaking from behind them, trying to cultivate an air of seniority. He gazed into the distance and forced a note of wonder into his voice.

'By this time tomorrow I'll be on my way to America.' He spoke carefully, as if awaiting a cue. 'Tomorrow,' he said. 'Tomorrow.'

Leila looked at him, but he continued to gaze studiously. Then, without announcement, he laughed, casually trying to change the tone of the conversation.

'Land of milk and honey! Land of plenty!' He turned to her.

'You know they can only say that if there's somewhere like us, you know, somewhere like here.'

He stopped playing with her hair and pointed his finger in the direction of the sand. Leila concentrated on concentrating on him.

'What I mean is, that for there to be a land of plenty there has to be a land of nothing, right?'

'Right,' said Leila, her eyes wide, her head nodding in agreement.

'Well, here it is. We living on it, or at least you still doing so, but all that can change, you know, but it's too dangerous to talk about it, especially not to them, my parents, your mother too. It's about us, our generation. There'll come a day when we can have the jobs in the town, when we can be making decisions, when we can run the country, our way! You, the brightest girl in the High School, you shouldn't be doing a clerical job, you should be studying, you should be coming to America too. You must be more forceful and make them realize how determined you are.' Leila nodded. 'I remember the time when you first tell me how you felt about this place but I bet you never tell anyone else?' Leila shook her head. 'You see what I mean? It's up to us, it must change. You must be true to your feelings about your country, no matter how critical they be.'

Arthur pushed his spectacles to a safer point further up his nose and he looked out to sea. Then he sprang to life again, the moonlight trapping the odd bits of dust in his hair.

'And you must understand how important it is that we get married.' Again Leila nodded. 'I mean, do you know the kind of future the two of us going to have when I get back from America? You know sometimes the prospects just frighten me. It's only two years, two years and I'll be qualified, and you'll have saved up some money, and after we marry we can have a baby, it's incredible. It's so straightforward, the future of these islands, this island, is in our hands, right here, now!'

Arthur stood up.

'There's a future here', he said, beginning the short walk down to the edge of the sea. 'A real future'.

Leila watched his every step as the darkness poured on to his body, reducing him to shadow and outline. She wanted him to leave in peace for she knew she would never wait for him, never think of him again after he had left in the morning, for simple dreams cluttered his mind. It was why he had achieved so much so soon and why she knew that ultimately he would achieve so little.

Leila noticed that Arthur's letter was now on the floor. They always looked the same in their long brown envelopes, his neat handwriting adorning the front, the carefully positioned stamp, always one stamp, in the top right-hand corner. What his letters lacked in variety they made up for in inaccuracy. 'Miss Leila Franks', always 'Miss Leila Franks'.

Millie came in and sat on the edge of the bed. She handed Leila a glass of water. Leila finished the water and Millie took the glass away into the front room. Leila wiped her mouth with the back of her hand and looked over the side of the bed to where the letter lay. His two years were almost up and he would soon be back. Two months, three months at the most.

'Come, get up,' said Millie, shouting through from the front room. 'No point in just lying in bed all day, for you never stop thinking of your mother that way. Why you don't do something? The house needs painting, you know that?'

Millie made Leila something to eat, then she and Leila sat on the doorstep. Millie held Shere carefully in her arms, a white cotton handkerchief protecting the child's head from the sun; Leila ate a large mango, the juice dribbling out and down the length of her arm. Leila was awake now and she tried not to think of Arthur's return: she had already thrown away his unread letter. Across the road and up towards the top end of the village, she saw two boys trying to kindle a reluctant afternoon fire in a square of charred bricks. Elsewhere she could see that others had been more successful as smoke rifled upwards from the many well-broomed backyards.

At this end of the village some boys were stoning the guava trees for fruit. A stone flew astray and nearly struck a small girl who stood barefoot at the stand-pipe filling her chipped enamel pail. She bent quickly and threw back a smooth pebble which dashed one of the boys on the shoulder. Then she turned and ran, water splashing up in all directions. The boys gave chase. The people of St Patrick's ignored the pandemonium. They had slopped out their hogs, spread the corn for their fowl and now they sat and watched their goats cutting the thin grass which sprouted idly along the verges and out from between the large stones in the many crumbling walls.

Leila heard the low buzzing of the bike. It became a roar, then a whine as Michael squeezed life into the brakes. Millie lifted her head from her daughter and squinted at him. Then she stood angrily and stared. She turned to go into the house but paused, waiting to see if Leila was going to follow. Clearly she was not. Millie stepped inside, closed the door and left Leila alone with her husband.

Michael kicked playfully at the dust.

'I come to see my child and to take him out for a ride in the fresh air if it's alright with you?'

Leila looked up at him. The same stocky build, the same neatness, the same smile; it was as if he had never been away.

Inside Millie stood, discarded. She listened hard, but there was a long silence in which neither Michael nor Leila spoke. Millie pulled Shere close and looked down at the sleeping Calvin, his mouth wet and dribbling, as if he was secretly eating something. His afternoon's rest was about to come to an end.

Leila lifted an arm to block out the sun so she could see Michael better.

'He don't going come to no harm,' said Michael. 'I just take him for a quick ride and come back so you don't have to worry.' He paused. 'It's my child too.'

82

'He'll soon be hungry,' said Leila.

'I soon come back with him. It's just a quick trip.'

Leila moved out of the sun and into the house. Millie was waiting, her feet stubbornly planted and splayed, Shere now thrown casually over her shoulder.

'Leila, you going let him have the child?'

Leila said nothing as she bent down and picked up Calvin.

'Leila, it's nearly six weeks since the child born. He can't just come and take it like that. He don't have no right to do so.'

Leila carried Calvin outside, wanting to get it over with as quickly as possible.

Michael wiped his damp hands on the back of his trousers and stretched out both his arms to receive his son. He held Calvin awkwardly.

'Please be careful with him,' whispered Leila.

Michael walked across the street to where the bike stood. He reached down and picked up a blue cotton jacket from off the seat. Then he laid Calvin on the seat and placed one hand on him to keep him balanced. He wriggled into the jacket, fastened the zip up a couple of inches, then slipped Calvin into the pouch he had just created. He zipped up the jacket halfway, and still supporting Calvin with one hand, he flipped his leg over the bike. Leila stood framed in the doorway. Behind her Millie touched her arm. They both turned and went inside.

When it had become clear that Michael had left her to live by Beverley, Leila had felt both relief and anguish. But in a place as small as St Patrick's it was her pride that had been hurt the most. However, those in the village looked upon her with sympathy and made it clear they knew she was in no way to blame for what had happened. If she ever wanted for anything she only had to ask.

But she had Millie, and with her help Leila had been slowly trying to regain some confidence. Then Calvin had been born and she felt he would need a father in a way in which she had not needed one, for he was a boy. She felt there would come a time, perhaps sooner than she dared think, when he would ask questions she could never answer, and seek company she might never be a part of. Leila knew, with Calvin's birth, that at some point Michael would probably reappear, and today it had happened.

He had a hold over her, and short of abandoning her son, Leila could see no way of correcting her mistake. Perhaps, as Millie had once said, she was a coward? Perhaps she had not made a mistake and things would sort themselves out? Perhaps, thought Leila, the same things had happened to her mother? As she began to cry, Millie hugged her. Then Leila's best friend wiped away a tear of her own.

Michael rode quickly but carefully to the far end of Sandy Bay. He kept one hand underneath Calvin and one hand remained on the handlebars. For the first mile or so Calvin cried, but as soon as he got used to the noise and the dust he was quiet, as if preparing himself for the next disruption. When they finally pulled up outside Beverley's house Michael dismounted and fished his son out from the warmth and security of his jacket. He took him sack-like in his arms and together they went inside.

No matter how bright it was outside, Beverley's house always looked dark. This made the furniture, which was uniformly wooden and chipped, look increasingly drab, especially as there was so little of it. Sometimes the room looked more like a discarded warehouse than a place for living in. As he came through the door the curtain at the far end of the room rippled gently. Behind it Michael could see that the bed was still unmade despite the fact that the afternoon was now full.

Beverley, her straightened hair newly starched and stiff, sat at the crooked table encouraging Ivor to eat some diced fruit from off a small metal spoon. He ate slowly, his jaws moving

84

rhythmically, and as he finished yet another laboured mouthful his mother turned around, her eyes tired and veined with blood. She saw the child. She turned back around and continued to feed Ivor. His fat mouth was dirty where his tongue had fought the spoon and spilled the fruit out on to his lips. It had slithered down his face to his chin where it lay plastered like a rich lumpy beard. Beverley licked the palm of her hand and shaved it clean. Her chest was numb with tension. As she scraped the spoon along the plate and pushed another hillock of food into her son's mouth she spoke, as if speaking to herself. 'Who tell you you can bring another child in here?'

Michael did not answer. Again she turned and looked at him as he stood in the doorway and played with Calvin's bare feet, the child's toes wriggling like small fish out of water. Beverley's breasts were too large for her body and any sudden movement created more movement. She saw little point in harnessing them in a brassière, and on days as hot as this one she simply opened her blouse and exposed her deep cleavage. She remained still, her freckled face tightening as her anger increased. Michael laughed quietly. 'I just wanted you to see my son.'

Having finished feeding Ivor, she stood and walked unhurriedly across to Michael, her every step measured, polite. She slapped him hard across the face, knocking him slightly off balance, then she spoke softly from between her teeth. 'Take the child out of my house.'

Outside a cockerel ran loose, the sun having stung its mind, and the untethered children laughed and fled. Ivor began to cry, but Beverley kept her eyes fixed firmly on Michael and the child. As Michael turned and left the house, his head still ringing, a scurrying, heat-blackened boy tripped headlong and fell at his feet. He looked up, his huge white eyes quickly filling with water, but Michael pushed past and left him basking in the dirt. The boy's knee was cut and bleeding and he began to cry. Beverley filled up a bowl with cold water so she could bathe the child's knee. Michael started up his bike. Again the crazed cockerel ran wild, but this time the bloodied boy did not flee. He pulled himself to his feet, then buried his wet face in his thin forearm and tried to keep the flying dust from Michael's bike out of his eyes.

Millie and Leila were once again sitting on the doorstep. They both tried hard to look unconcerned as he got off the bike. He took Calvin from his jacket and Leila rescued her child. Millie stared hard at Michael who avoided her eyes. Neither of them said anything to him so he left, his gait for once clumsy and uncomfortable. As soon as the sound of the bike had drained away Leila began to examine Calvin as if convinced that she had been given the wrong child. Millie looked across at her. Leila stood up and carried Calvin inside, her cheeks hot with shame.

When Michael got back to Beverley's house the door was, for the first time ever, locked. He knocked repeatedly, but short of breaking it down there was no way in. For a moment he thought, then he climbed on his bike and sped down the road towards Baytown where Beverley spent most afternoons selling fruit, or else sitting by the side of the road sewing some garment. But when Michael saw her she was walking. He roared past, braked to a halt, then slowly turned his bike around. Beverley walked towards him, stopped and sat calmly on the grass verge. She draped her tired son across her knees so he hung like a sagging washing line. Michael dismounted and stood before her. She refused to look up at him. Above them neither cloud nor bird stirred.

'You lock the door,' he said.

Ivor looked up at his father, but his mother said nothing.

'I said, you lock the door and I want to know why it is you done so.'

Beverley would not look up at him. Then, as if from nowhere, a car skidded furiously around the corner and into sight. It sounded its horn as it passed by, riding the heat waves away into the country. Michael followed the car until it passed out of sight, but Beverley refused to look. Michael took an exasperated step backwards as if ready to leave. Then he paused and spat at her, but the spittle got caught at the corners of his mouth and just dribbled down on to his shirt. Beverley still refused to look up at him. Michael ran his shirt sleeve across his lips, then turned and walked back to his bike. He leaped on to it and rode away from her and the boy for good.

The wind whipped into his face and his ears were blocked up with the noise of the bike. As Michael leaned first into, then out of the noose-like twists and turns in the road, he saw life flickering by like a speed-crazed movie. The braver children waved while the normal ones stood open-mouthed and watched. Ivor would be normal, like her. He even looked like her. Sometimes he could not believe that such a blank child could have anything to do with him, its eyes dull, its movements already full of well-rehearsed sloth. He roared on, then in his anger he wrestled the bike to the side of the road and walked down the hill towards the sea. He stood and looked, as he had stood and looked many times before, and he tried to get Beverley out of his spinning mind, but he kept remembering.

Beverley had sat in the doorway, her recently pregnant bulk preventing the sun from streaming in. He had sat at the table eating alone, as usual. Having finished his food he dismissed the fork with a rude clatter and stared at the woman's rounded back. Two days earlier he had seen the fat envelope by the bed, half-hidden under a glass jar clouded with cotton wool. He had picked it up, looked at it and seen that its postmark was from America, its contents American dollar bills. Clearly her husband had written to her, but Beverley had not mentioned it.

As the afternoon slowed in deference to the day's heat, he had watched a thin line of dampness appear on the back of her loose blouse, closely following the slight curvature of her spine. Then, against his will, she slept. On awakening she immediately looked to see if Michael was still there. He seemed to her as though he was sleeping, but he must have felt her stare, for he glanced up and their tired eyes met.

'I have something in the yard for you,' said Beverley, her speech slow and slightly slurred. 'I meant to give it to you earlier.' Sure that he would follow, but in his own time, she stood and began to make her way around the side of the house.

The bike was secondhand, but it looked like the sort of bike Michael had always wanted. He stared at Beverley, then at the bike, then back again at Beverley who was standing in the yard letting the flies walk about on her face, letting them lick her full lips and bathe in the corners of her eyes. She stood in a heat-induced misery, a tragically becalmed figure, offering Michael her gift of a motorbike like a naked mother offers her worn-out body to a drunken overseer. He had wanted to say something, but every time he looked from her to the bike, and back again to her, he became increasingly angry, for in her eyes, in every line of her face he could see the full confession of her servility. He had finally looked away, wanting to see neither woman nor bike. In the corner of the yard, and leaning up against a rusty butter tin, stood a blunt stave. He needed only to take the one step, bend forward slightly, and it was his; but the newborn child cried out from inside the house and Beverley flinched. She searched Michael's rigid face. Then a thought as quiet as a cloud crashed in her mind. She followed his eyes to the stave and realized he might beat her. Their child cried on. She tried to sneak away from Michael, but it was stupid, for she knew that he was aware of what she was doing. So she turned and walked back around the front of the house and slammed the door behind her. Then she pushed up a chair to the door and went to see the child.

Michael had climbed on to the bike. He had practised for a while, thrusting power into it, letting it surge, slipping on the brakes, treating it like an unbroken animal. Then he kicked open the gate and took off toward St Patrick's where he would pick up his future wife, take her to Black Rocks, then sleep. His head was spinning then as it did now.

The cold breeze dampened as it began to hold the rougher evening spray. Then the dusk fell and Michael stood, the white edge of the sea threatening his feet. He watched the strengthening foam surging towards him. Purposefully, almost stubbornly, he waited until the sea had gathered enough energy to roll gently across his feet before turning and making his tired way back up the hill to his bike. Some of the spittle was still on his shirt. He quickly wiped it off, then spat, properly.

His grandmother was sitting in the doorway, her bare legs jutting out stiff from underneath her blue dress. She saw Michael but said nothing in reply to his 'hello'. She leaned to one side and let him pass. As he did so he gently squeezed her shoulder, but his touch was unsure and tense, and his grandmother knew he intended to stay a while. It was more a gesture of arrival than a greeting. She listened as he slipped quietly into his bedroom.

Michael lay on the bed trying hard to feel calm and peaceful. Then he rolled over and the dust which hung in the air shook. He could not sleep or rest, even, his mind still speeding.

*

Two weeks later Leila woke early and prepared a warm bath for Calvin. Millie sat peacefully by the door, holding the sleeping Shere. Across the street the morning light played on the naked bodies of the children. Behind them, rising in mystic spirals, span the greyish mist of burning rubbish. Millie's still half-closed face welcomed the sly seduction of the cool breeze and soon she was asleep again, her head bobbing slightly but her child warm and safe in her arms. Inside Leila dried Calvin slowly, as if smoothing off the edges on a precious piece of wooden sculpture. Then she laid him on his back to rest, his tiny arms and legs sternly erect, scaffold-like, as if waiting for a cloth covering. Leila stood back and sighed, her body graceful and slender like a palm, but on her brow she wore the whorls and curls of a much stouter, a more mature tree.

A boy of about twelve, dressed in short khaki pants which were neatly torn in a tight curve across the full breadth of his backside, let his ancient bicycle smash to the ground. He ran past the now awakening Millie and into the house. Leila looked up, but before she could speak he began to gasp his garbled message.

'Miss Millie must come quick – now – her Aunt Toosie, she dead.'

Millie stood and turned her back to the road. She stepped forward into the house. Panic clung to the boy's sticky face. He nervously crooked his leg and rubbed the itchy sole of one foot on the narrow calf of the other. Leila poured him a glass of coconut water and pressed it into his hand, but his fidgety eyes were now fixed on Millie whose mouth hung open, wide and dry.

*

Three days later the funeral took place. For those who had known her it was a sad Sunday morning but, as expected, the turn-out was more than respectable. In fact the funeral would be talked about for weeks, maybe months. It was the sign of a good death, and a good life.

In the afternoon Bradeth and Millie and Leila and the two babies made their slow way up to St Patrick's. When they arrived back Shere and Calvin were laid inside away from the sun, and the three adults sat outside and drank iced water. Eventually, after an uneasy silence, they climbed into the conversation they knew they would have to have, but which none of them wanted to initiate. It was Bradeth who made the first move.

'I decide to marry to Millie and we going back to live in Sandy Bay where we going try and build up Millie's Aunt Toosie's old shop.'

Again there was silence. Bradeth kicked at the dust, more in exasperation than exhaustion, satisfied he had at least made an effort. Leila looked over at Millie, who in turn took a drink of water, then tucked her knees up under her chin.

'I'm happy for you both,' said Leila, leaning over and kissing her friend lightly on the cheek.

Millie smiled quickly, then began to speak.

'I think,' she hesitated, 'we both of us may be feeling a little guilty about leaving you and Calvin up here on your own.'

Leila laughed. 'It's alright, don't worry about me. You'll soon be married and you have a beautiful daughter and now a shop. I think you have enough to be worrying about.'

'But,' stuttered Bradeth, 'you have any idea of what it is you going do? I mean, you feel you can manage?'

Leila spoke quickly as if making it up on the spur of the moment. 'I think I'm going to England.'

'When you decide this?' asked Millie, her voice full of disbelief.

'A few days ago.'

Again it went quiet and the noises of the street filled their heads. Bradeth scratched desperately at a small callus on his knuckle, convinced that there was some easier, less painful way of getting across their simple decision to Leila. Millie spoke hurriedly, only confirming what he felt.

'Well, till you go you realize that we still want to do all we can to help, and one of us will be up by you every day to check if things is alright.'

Feeling unable to survive another lull in the conversation, Leila stood up to go inside.

'I thought I heard Calvin crying.' Nobody answered her so she left the two of them sitting in the sun.

Millie's hushed voice darted through the air. 'We can't just leave her on her own with the child.'

Bradeth flicked the lump of hardened skin up and into the air. 'Well, it's you who say she don't want to come and stay by us in Sandy Bay.'

'As long as she have her health there's nothing going to take her out of her mother's house.' They were both silent, hoping that Leila could not hear them. Then Bradeth spoke. 'I think I going see Michael again. He can't just keep on treating her this way, like she don't exist or nothing.' He paused. 'Maybe he change a little?'

'Maybe he grown two heads,' snapped Millie. 'And besides that, man have to change more than a bit. Too much proud father on this island with invisible baby.' Bradeth listened to Millie's anger but he was not following her words.

'I going fetch him,' he said reflectively. 'Tell Leila I gone off to move some stuff from the shop or something.' He threw back his drink and stood up. 'I see you later.'

Bradeth kissed Millie on the top of her head and walked back down the road in search of a lift. Leila came out just as Bradeth was disappearing into the bend. She held Calvin in her arms and followed Bradeth around the corner and out of sight, her mouth and eyes working separately. 'Calvin's too restless to sleep.'

Michael was not at Beverley's. The door was open but nobody responded to Bradeth's shouting. It seemed like the place had been deserted, and the children stared at him as if astonished that he expected to find it any other way. Bradeth strode up towards the other side of Sandy Bay. He found Michael sitting on his grandmother's step, tossing pebbles at an imaginary target. Uncharacteristically Michael had on a straw hat which was perched uneasily on the back of his head. The beads of perspiration queuing up around his temples and his brow suggested that he had been sat in the sun tossing pebbles for some time. Michael looked up but he continued to lob the small missiles at the target, wildly and without precision, memory being now his sole guide.

'I come to have a talk,' said Bradeth, hitching up his trousers and tightening his belt two notches. Michael smiled into his friend's face.

'Well, talk then.'

'I soon marrying to Millie,' he began, 'and we going to take over the shop now Toosie dead.' He paused, hoping that Michael would say something, but he did not.

'Your wife going be alone and she have a child, your child.'

Bradeth felt as if he was talking to himself, for Michael still tossed his idle pebbles. He spoke again, this time gesturing angrily with his hands.

'I mean, you thinking of going back to she or what it is you playing at, man? You think you come fucking clever, eh?'

Michael crooked his head so that the frayed edges of his straw hat slatted the smaller rays of the sun which fell through it. He threw down his pebbles and stood up.

'I not playing at anything, what you playing at?'

'I playing at being a friend to your wife. Either you go round there and be a husband for she or I telling you not to bother to go see she at all, for I won't stand by and see you treating her to all this coming and going and coming and going shit.'

'You telling me what to do?' asked Michael.

Bradeth spat his answer. 'I telling you I going break every bone in your damn body if you don't start treating she right. Every last bone.'

Michael stared back hard, unblinking, so Bradeth, lips drawn tight, continued, 'We going have to finish off this friendship unless you listen to what I saying, and I telling you that as a man, and I mean it.'

They stared at each other, then Michael sat. He thought for a while then spoke without looking up. 'I going see she later.'

Bradeth looked down at the rough circle of his friend's straw hat and he breathed out, hard and long, but as quietly as possible.

After Millie had left, Leila put Calvin to sleep. Then she sat on a stool and looked at some of her mother's old letters. Though the daylight was almost spent she wanted to read by what little there was. She was only halfway through the pile when she heard a light tapping at the door. Michael opened it without waiting for an answer, then entered confidently, as if arriving for a pre-arranged appointment.

'I thought maybe we could have a talk.' He sat down opposite her, but his chair was a little unbalanced and it surprised him. He should have remembered.

'Bradeth tell me that he going marry to Millie and he's worried about you being on your own.' Michael paused, but Leila said nothing. Then the words just fell limply from his mouth.

'I been staying down by my grandmother and I want to come back to stay by you.' Again he paused, but there seemed little point in stopping now. 'I think I should try and make it work for the both of us, and for the sake of the child.

Leila blinked, her eyes tiring in the now fast-dying light. Her skin felt sticky.

'You said that before.'

There followed a long pause in which neither could look at the other.

'I want you back.'

'I never went away, Michael.'

'I want to come back, don't you understand what I'm saying?'

'I understand, but . . .' Leila paused. 'I married you in a church, not under a bush.'

Michael dropped his eyes before he spoke.

'I understand. I really do. You're my wife, Leila.'

Leila listened to him, realizing he was speaking to her as if he were telling her something she did not know.

They lay in bed. Leila had moved Calvin's cot into her mother's room, though it was still cluttered with Millie's jars and combs and brushes. Then, having waited until they were next to each other, she told Michael what she imagined Bradeth had probably not told him. She told him that she was going to England to be with her mother. Michael turned to face her and he held her hand tightly. Maybe as a family it was what they needed? There was work there, wasn't there? And there was opportunity? His wife looked at him. They could talk about it tomorrow, for she knew Michael did not understand her or her desire to escape the life she was trapped in. And, as she looked at Michael, she saw him still as both a destroyer and a partner, but she knew that he too would come to England because Calvin needed a father, and because she did not want her mother to see her as having failed in something she did not wish her to partake of in the first place. But if the marriage did fail again in England, thought Leila, it would not be her fault. Nobody could blame her. Her mother would see that for herself.

Leila fell asleep on her stomach, her arm draped lifelessly over Michael's still heaving chest. Then Calvin began to cry and Michael had to wake her up.

*

Michael turned off Island Road and rode into the slightly broader main street of the capital. It was a while since he had been to town, but now that he was here the first thing he noticed was that Baytown seemed somehow deserted, especially for a Saturday. No longer was it the familiar crowded chaos, it was more like a mid-American town similar to those in the old western films they had sent down from America once every month, or every two months, that both young and old queued for hours to see.

He slowed up, avoiding some goats in the street, and parked his bike outside the Day to Dawn bar. Michael dusted himself down. He took off his sunglasses, pushed them into his top pocket and looked at the half dozen or so goats which continued to wander free. Before long someone would come to coax them from the road, for at the moment neither car nor bus could pass safely. Up above the sun burned fiercely and Michael's shadow was short and stunted. He drew the back of his hand across his dry lips where some grit had crept.

Across the road two boys stood in a large island of shadow cast down by an overhanging tree. A pair of bad men leaning up against a store front, one knee drawn up, foot flat back against the wall, sucking slowly at their shaved ices. They watched him hard, young boys playing tough, then Michael laughed at them and they straightened up, shoulders hunched, teeth bared. The shorter of the two boys threw his shaved ice dramatically to the ground, then faltered and let his eyes drop after it wishing he had not done so. Again Michael laughed as the taller of the two dug his elbow into his friend's side as if to say, 'Why you do that, man?' The shorter boy snapped around and sucked his teeth. Michael left the two of them arguing and made his way into the bar.

Inside the Day to Dawn things were even quieter. Both juke box and radio were silent, as if dead, and barman apart there was nobody else in the place. Michael slapped down 50 cents on the wooden bar top. The barman continued to dry his glass, polishing it like it was a priceless family heirloom, then he threw the towel back over his shoulder and put the glass down to one side.

'Is an eye-opener you want?' Michael nodded. The man reached for a bottle, broke off the cap, then slopped the contents into an oversized glass.

'First drink of the day always the sweetest,' he said, sliding the beer a couple of feet along the bar and hoping it would pull up before Michael. It did. Happy with himself, he scratched the 50 cents back up off the top of the bar. It used to be a thick plank of freshly varnished and uniformly dark wood, but now it was lacerated with light scratches of differing depths to match the barman's shifting moods.

'So what happen? We don't be seeing so much of you down here these days. You staying up back of island now Bradeth move out of town?'

Michael drank deeply, emptying the glass in one, then nodded more out of courtesy than interest.

'So you come country boy for true! Country boy come to town!'

The barman peeled back his lips like the lid of an old piano, and his teeth played a friendly mocking tune. He picked up Michael's glass, rinsed it in a murky bowl of water, then pulled the towel down from his shoulder and began to dry it.

'So you come country boy!' he laughed. Then, without warning, he leaned forward and spoke softly as if conveying a secret piece of wisdom. 'Though they do say if a tree fall over in the forest the others do prop it up. You fall over down here and there be nobody to prop you up and nobody to pick you up either. I planning on going back country myself.' He paused for a moment, then went on, 'I work so damn hard down here I sure one of these days I going run my blood to water.'

Michael drummed his fingers lightly against the top of the bar and nodded. 'I don't blame you, man. I don't blame you at all.'

He looked closely at the barman's face, noticing the veins around his temples, like branches from an old tree. In them he saw the hopeless truth. The man could no more return to the country than Michael could run a bar. It was too late. The man continued to dry the glass.

'I going now,' said Michael, backing off from the bar. 'I going see you later.'

The barman just nodded, then he put down the glass and scratched his head, wondering what it was he had said to drive Michael away. After a while he gave up. Everyone knew the boy had his funny ways.

The ground was stained with a dark wetness where the shaved ice had melted, but the two boys had gone. Michael began the long slow walk down to the market, edging his way along the narrow and carelessly defined streets. Up above the gulls circled, and to them Baytown must have looked like a hot corrugated iron sea. Michael pressed on, trying not to look at the defeated faces that lined these streets, men in grease-stained felt hats and women in deceptively gay bandannas, their eyes glazed, arms folded, standing, leaning, resting up against the zinc fencing of their front yards, their children playing, racing scraps of wood in the liquid sewage, but the walk only seemed to get longer.

Though still a way off, Michael could smell the fresh fish and the tangy fruit of the market, and he could feel the growing piles of discarded rubbish under his feet. Then a ringing voice sang out above the buzzing silence of the day, and the man ran towards him, eyes bright, arms flapping wildly, shirt hanging adrift and brazen, detached from his trousers.

'Michael man, Michael! Where you going?'

The man was short and stocky. He looked wildly about himself like an animal caught in a steel trap. He skidded to a halt and began to splutter, letting his lower lip hang loose so Michael could see the bright redness of his gums against the pink of his tongue.

'Well, man, what you doing?'

Michael shook his limp hand. 'I just going pick up some yams and thing for Leila.'

'Well, I surprise to see you for I hear the pair of you done gone off to England like the rest of the dámn island. Boy, I sure you gone, you know. I sure, sure.'

'Next Thursday,' said Michael, eager to escape the man's enthusiasm.

'Boy, you gone on next Thursday boat then?'

'Yes, man.'

'Well, then what I hear is half-true. You really going England, you really going.'

He said nothing more and for a few moments he just looked Michael up and down in boyish admiration. Then his eyes flashed and he licked his eager lips. 'And you still has the bike and everything?'

'Yes, man.'

'Same Michael, same Michael.' He paused, then snapped to life again. 'Hey! I just think of something. You remember Footsie Walters' brother, Alphonse?'

'I hear talk of him.'

'Well, you know he just come back from England? I sure he going be able to tell you lots of things about the place that you don't going get to hear from nobody else for everybody be too much hearsay and hesay.'

Michael looked at this man as he hopped from foot to foot, unburnt energy coursing through his every muscle. He was in his early twenties, Michael's own age, and he helped out on the fishing boats, begging a drink here, a piece of food there. To most people he was simply a young man who had as yet no life of his own to recount in exchange for his scraps of food, no stories of the sea and far away places, no wars that he had fought, no bridges that he had built, rivers he had forded, or canals he had dug. Thoughts of who he was, and why he was living as he did, were beyond him. He lived and that was all. Once, a long time ago now, some white man had called him the conscience of the island and he had laughed loud, then begged a next piece of bread.

'Where Alphonse Walters living now?' asked Michael.

'Just down by the water's edge. Ask for him there, this side of the big boats. You want me come with you?'

Michael shook his head, pushed ten cents into the man's palm and walked off.

'Mr Preston, for a ten cents more I can go watch your bike for you.'

Michael ignored him and walked on.

Alphonse Walters lived in a flimsy one-roomed shack called a house. His hushed voice crept through the stillness encouraging Michael to enter. He did so and sat nervously, for the man's burnt orange-brown skin was rich and leathery, as if ready to be stripped clear of his body and moulded into a saddle. It was like nothing Michael had ever seen before. His hair was black and greasy and flecked at the edges with a light grey, and below it protruded a pair of bright, but sad, dark brown eyes set in hungry, uneven sockets so that Michael had the triple impression of depth, wonder and poverty. When he spoke he did so quickly, letting his head drop to one side like a floppy dog's, throwing out a helpless arm, palm turned up, to make important points. He shrugged his shoulders a lot, and sometimes he clasped his thigh and walked blindly and with an exaggerated limp to emphasize the point about his lost ship and how he got to England. Then he made a violent downward jabbing of the hand meant to symbolize a customs officer in England stamping his non-existent passport, and he laughed loudly at this private joke.

'You know what lathe is, boy? When I first get to England I work with more lathes than there be people on this island, you can believe that? And the thing is, they be all in one room and when they start up they make such a damn noise that all I hear is the sea.'

His laughter cracked, then split. He coughed violently, trying to catch his breath, then he continued.

'Only one day I did listen too hard and the noise sound like the world done finish, or me at least. What happen is I knock over some acid which spray up all over me.' He paused for a moment. 'I been noticing how you looking at me skin funny so, but now you know. They give me £100 and tell me to go home, but I stay another five years just doing nothing, boy, begging in truth. But now I back home and you can see how I living.' Again he laughed as he remembered, but every word was measured, painful.

'You must be careful in England. Concentrate. I remember one day in England I see a man in the street so lonely he just fall over, wet his pants, laugh, then cry. Then I see some policemen come to arrest him but I don't know what for. Maybe he drunk in charge of a sidewalk?' He lowered his eyes. 'They probably take him somewhere and mash him up a little, then let the man go.' Again he paused. 'You must be careful, for it's a stupid and bad, crazy world, Michael. You say is Michael your name, yes?'

'Michael.'

'Michael,' he mused. 'I still can't place your people, but if they die in the boat then I suppose I wouldn't have get to know them.'

He stopped for a moment and thought of the boat disaster. Then he lifted his face to Michael.

'But I don't care what anyone tell you, going to England be good for it going raise your mind. For a West Indian boy like you just being there is an education, for you going see what England do for sheself and what she did do for you and me here and everyone else on this island and all the other islands. It's a college for the West Indian.'

Michael listened for hours, the voice small, eventually weakening and giving up altogether, but not before it had cleared out the old man's mind of all the things that England had meant to him, all the things that he had seen, that he had felt, that he had lived. For Michael it had been like eavesdropping on a cold and chilly dream.

In the half-light of sunset Michael stood and pressed a dollar (all the money that he had) into the rusty palm of the man. He left the house to find his motorbike. As he climbed on he realized who it was the man reminded him of. Like his grandfather, the man had filled his head with ideas, half-formed, half-truths, uncritical, myth, none of which could be verified except by trust. He turned his bike towards St Patrick's.

The following afternoon their guests arrived complete with a tired baby and a carrier bag crammed full with bottles of beer. Leila and Michael sat outside and watched them coming up the road, the last few yards seemingly endless. Millie led the way in her blue dress and white hat, her white shoes, white handbag and the bottles of beer to match. Bradeth looked equally smart in his suit, the same suit he had worn to the wedding, even though the pants were beginning to bulge a little at the knees and drop at the crotch. The jacket had never really fitted. The two of them, husband towering over wife-to-be and carrying the sleeping child, looked exhausted.

Millie put down the beer, the bottles clanking angrily, not caring whether or not they smashed. She reached across for Shere and followed Leila into the house.

'I tell him we should get a taxi or wait on a bus, for Shere wants to sleep, but will he listen? 'We going walk for it's a nice cool day,' he says, and on top of that he turn up at the damn church carrying a bag full of beer and the minister calling the banns.' She sucked her teeth long and hard. 'When he say if anyone know of any just cause or impediment, or whatever it is they say, I nearly die for I beginning to think of a few myself.'

Leila played with her god-daughter's small and sticky hand. Then she moved over to the tap and started to run some water into a bowl.

Outside Bradeth remained standing. He scratched his bristled head and looked down at his friend.

'You want one, take one,' he said, pointing at the beer. 'I think I done fetch enough for the afternoon.'

Michael stretched forward, picked one out, opened it and handed it to Bradeth. Then he opened one for himself. Bradeth hitched up his trousers and sat down beside Michael, his knees shooting up past his ears. He took a long drink before venturing to turn to him and speak.

'So tell me,' he said, 'How is everything? It's all working out?' Michael nodded. 'It seem like it,' said Bradeth. 'Leila looking better already.'

Michael took a long and satisfied drink, then closed his eyes. They sat like this for a few minutes and then, without opening his eyes, Michael began to speak.

'We not buying no return, you know. We both decide it's a new life for us over there so we just going come back when we come back. Not enough space to grow or do things here.' He paused. 'But you know what it is I talking about.'

'Yes, man,' said Bradeth. 'I know what it is you saying.'

'It's just that I don't want to spend the rest of my life looking for small work when I know I can get big work if I wants it. Me, I want a car and a big house and a bit of power under my belt, like any man does want. This country breed too many people who just cut cane in season and happy to be rum-jumbie out of it.'

'It's true,' said Bradeth, 'but what you think if say next year Millie and myself decide we going come to England?'

Michael laughed and opened his eyes. 'I don't see nothing wrong but you must first ask Millie.'

Bradeth sucked his teeth. 'Well, I don't know what she thinking, but if we come it means she going have to sell up the shop and I somehow don't think she going want to do that.'

'Well, maybe you better ask she for you can never tell.' Michael paused for a moment, then went on, 'And you hear we have a buyer for the house now. When Leila's mother come back she going build a new house further back off the road for some peace.'

'You got it all organized.'

103

'You have to, man. You have to.'

Bradeth leaned forward and pulled another two bottles from the bag. He opened them, passed one to Michael and they continued to drink. Leila came out of the house.

'The food is going to be ready in about ten minutes. Do you want anything?'

They both made noises which meant they did not, and Leila went back inside. For a moment they were quiet again. Then Michael spoke. 'So when you going tell she you want to go to England?'

'I don't know as yet. I don't know how she going take it so I have to pick my time.'

They drank silently, then opened their third bottles. Bradeth turned to his friend.

'I hear about one coloured man out there who writing home saying he be having at least three or four different white girls a week.'

'He lie.'

'I tell you like I hear it.'

'I know the man?'

'It's Willie Daniels' cousin from Halfway House. He writing back every month and sending postal orders for the other three Williams brothers to come out one by one.'

'He must have a good job, then.'

'They say every coloured man in England have a good job that can pay at least $100 a week.'

'Yes, I hear about it but I'm not sure,' said Michael.

'Well, you know Shorty Fredrick's son out there now making a fortune from investments, and you remember what Shorty Fredricks' son was back here? The man born a criminal thief and alcoholic.'

'I hear about him and a few of the others.'

'So life over there can be good, you know. I mean real good, man, and you lucky, you know.'

Bradeth's adrenalin began to surge and he laughed. He

was excited. Michael drained his bottle, then looked at his friend.

'You know you start thinking that way, man, and you might end up selling your pants to a white man.' Michael kicked the dust. 'And that's the truth, for yesterday Alphonse Walters, brother to Footsie, almost tell me as much. He tell me sometimes England don't be no joke for a coloured man.'

Bradeth emptied his bottle, thought hard, then spoke. He avoided Michael's gaze.

'I sure that what he tell you be true, but I suppose the only way to find out is to go there.'

Michael nodded and they were quiet. After a minute or so Leila shouted from inside the house that the food was ready, and Michael rubbed some life back into his face. Before they went in Bradeth picked up an extra couple of bottles to drink with the food, then he dragged the bag into the shade. They would drink the rest later.

After the meal they sat outside again, this time with Leila and Millie. Inside the children were awake, but lying contentedly by themselves away from the heat. Millie talked about the banns and went over the horrors of the service again. And Bradeth praised the food endlessly. And then they were quiet, as if running out of topics to talk about. Eventually Millie, squinting into the sun, turned to Leila and spoke softly, but with an accusatory innocence. 'So who else you know in England beside your mother?'

Leila thought for a moment. 'Only people you hear about, or people we talk about.'

Millie turned to Michael. 'And what about yourself?'

'Same as Leila.' He paused. 'I mean, you know people from time who you know gone there but you not real friends with them so you don't keep no address or nothing.'

Bradeth chipped in, 'Anyway, it's the type of place in which I hear you soon going make friends.'

Millie was swift in picking this up. 'Who tell you so?'

105

Bradeth shrugged his shoulders and Millie went on, 'You not hear about the woman who think things getting so bad over there that she send all her precious belongings and a family photograph album to an address in America and she don't even know no people there. She just make up an address in New York for she sure that England going put all coloureds in concentration camps and she want something to survive. You tell me that does sound like a friendly place to you?'

Bradeth shifted uneasily. 'I hear the woman mad,' he said.

Millie laughed scornfully. 'You think so? I hear it's a two-week crossing on some stink-up Italian boat stopping at every damn port except Tokyo and Russia, and the only food I do hear they give you is cheap rum that sure to kill you dead, and everyone running like their arse catch-a-fire.'

Leila coughed, then spoke. 'People are always saying all kinds of different things.'

But Millie was adamant. 'Too many people beginning to act like it's a sinful thing to want to stay on this island but there don't be no law which say you must go to England, you know. People here too much follow-fashion.' Leila did not have time to answer. 'So Michael, why you don't say something? You being too damn quiet for my reasoning.'

'Well, I think you right some of the way but I don't think it can be anything but good for a young family. I mean there is where all the opportunity is, and it don't mean to say we can't come back here with some profits after we finish working over there if it's so we choose to do.'

Millie was quick to speak again. 'So just tell me how many people you see coming back from England with anything except the clothes they standing up in?'

'No, Millie, it's not fair.' Michael wanted to get up to make his point but he remained seated. 'People only been going out there a few years so why they should be coming back now? It's just starting.'

'So how long you think it going take them before they coming back?' asked Millie.

'Well, for those that really want to come back maybe five years,' suggested Michael. 'Maybe ten.'

Millie laughed and everyone went quiet.

'More like five hundred years,' she said. 'Maybe longer.'

Again they fell into a deep silence, each daring one of the others to speak first. Then Michael started up the conversation on a different topic. For the next two hours they talked of anything, everything, but nothing to do with England. That subject just caused too much trouble among friends.

*

Thursday morning and the restless sun rose particularly early, or so it seemed. Michael opened his eyes and reached over to touch his wife, but his blind hand slid across the sheet and off the end of the bed. He turned over, sat up and heard her talking to Calvin. She was packing. In the pale morning light Michael's shadow moved slowly across the greyish white slats of the bedroom wall. He decided to lie in bed a few moments longer. As he reached down to pull up the sheet, he caught his hand in a band of light which clipped the edge of the ring; his memory stirred.

Last night he had eaten his meal in silence, then, scraping the wooden chair across the floor, he moved over to sit in the cooling breeze of the open doorway and watch the evening fall. Leila cleared up the soiled plate and utensils from the small table top. Michael kneaded his soft palm into his face, wondering whether he should bother to shave before he left but, as ever, there was very little stubble to remove. In this light nobody would notice. Leila handed her husband an open bottle of beer which he drank slowly and reflectively before placing it down empty beside the chair.

'Anything you want?' asked Leila.

'No, it's alright.'

Michael spoke to her with detachment. Up above a solitary gull wheeled lazily. Then the sun set, not with the usual outburst of colour, but with a gentle, almost touching grace.

'Leaving this place going make me feel old, you know, like leaving the safety of your family to go live with strangers,' said Michael.

Leila stood up and carried Calvin across to the table where she would finally prepare him for bed. She looked across at the back of Michael's head, feeling as though he were confessing something to her and that perhaps she should not have moved away from him. But before she had a chance to say anything, he spoke again.

'I met Footsie Walters' brother Alphonse in town last Saturday when I went in to carry the yams. He don't make it sound bad or nothing, but he make it sound a bit different from how I did imagine it.'

'Which is like what?'

'Better, I suppose.'

For a moment Leila had thought she must be mistaken. She wondered if Michael was consciously trying to create this mood or if he had really forgotten himself. Either way she went forward and put a hand on to his shoulder.

'I know things between us don't be so good at times,' he said, looking up at her, 'but it's like you're putting a chicken into a cardboard box. The thing bound to start jumping about a bit and loose off a few feathers.' He laughed, then scraped back his chair and stood up. 'I'm beginning to sound like a preacher man.'

He fastened his shirt buttons up to his neck, rolled his cuffs down and buttoned them up, then he quickly slipped on his blue suit jacket. He dragged his chair back across the floor and left it by the table. Michael kissed his son lightly on the forehead and did the same to his wife. He knew they would be asleep by the time he returned.

For what he imagined to be the last time Michael pulled up outside her parched house. The bleached and peeling walls looked uncomfortable, being nothing more than a set of ill-matching strips that had been nailed together in a seemingly random pattern, but his grandfather's building skills, however limited, had stood the test of time. The door was slightly ajar, an open invitation to either a friend or a member of the family. Michael, his pulse still racing from the journey, eased himself down from off the bike and quickly climbed up the slow step and into the house.

His grandmother sat facing him. Her legs were hopelessly bowed, her thick varicose veins running up and down their bruised and stubby length. Her face was silent and black, blank, neither eyes nor mouth willing to capitulate to movement or betray emotion. She sat placidly, and in her gnarled hands she held something tight in an obvious attempt to conceal it from Michael who, as yet, could not see what it was. This slightly hostile, but never threatening confrontation was reassuringly familiar to Michael. He closed the door behind him, safe in the knowledge that there could be nothing seriously amiss.

Slightly to his grandmother's right, and to Michael's left, was a small, rickety-looking chair which he was clearly expected to occupy. He sat and waited. She looked at him, her eyes small, imprecise, grey, like those of dead fish, but he could not look back at her for long without having to turn aside and fix his eyes upon the dusty unswept floor. She said nothing. After a few moments his eyes began to wander, stealthily at first, and then with a greater boldness, passing over the photographs, the piles of old crushed letters, the heavy oak sideboard, the light cane baskets, the heavy iron pots, the broken wireless, all yellowing in their resting places.

Then, as the silence deepened, he stole a glance at his grandmother. These days she occupied her house as one would occupy a waiting room. She spoke in a whisper.

'So it's tomorrow you going?'

'Yes.'

Michael shifted slightly, the low creaking of his chair sounding unpleasant in his ears, but she did not take her eyes from him.

'You thinking of coming back?'

'I think so, but I don't know when.'

'I don't care about when, all I want to know is if you thinking of coming back.'

He paused then answered, his voice modest.

'I'm thinking of coming back, but I'm not sure if I will.'

'I see.'

Her Bible was on a small table by her side, something to lean on, and she stole a reassuring glance in its direction. Her austerity was not merely as a result of poverty.

'You been like a son to me since your parents die and I have a lot of hope invested in you, boy. I don't want you to fail.'

Without taking her eyes from Michael, she slowly stretched her fingers like a crab flexing its legs.

'Take this with you.'

Carefully balanced between her forefingers and her thumbs was a plain gold band. It looked like a wedding ring. She held out her hands and Michael leaned forward and took it. He looked down at the ring, not knowing whether to slip it on to his finger or just hold it. So he held it, and as he did so he listened; only now did he become conscious of the crickets whose noisy chorus had been with him the whole time. Their multiple voices spat, crackled, whistled, almost daring him to leave the house and come out and join them.

'Go now and don't forget what I tell you. Have yourself a good life and take good care of your girl and child. I say girl for she still young but she can help you to a good life if you treat

110

her right.' She paused, then with the smallest of movements she nodded, as if trying to warn him of some fast-approaching danger.

'She can help you.'

Michael felt an uneasy smile twist his lips, but clearly his grandmother had nothing further to say. She closed her eyes to him, then slowly re-formed her hands in the centre of her lap with all the deliberation of a leaf curling at its edges. Michael rose, his shadow rushing before him, and he moved across to the door. Quietly, not wishing to disturb his grandmother, he pulled it to and stood nervously in the moonlight.

Above him the trees rustled; he listened as a stray dog barked timidly. Trapped by a thousand chains the bad dogs howled back, long and deep. Then it was quiet again, just the crickets, the leaves and the wind; even the sea seemed stilled and worried, deliberately secretive. Michael dug into his jacket pocket and fumbled for the gold band. He slipped it on to the third finger of his right hand. It fitted perfectly and would remain there.

A cloud quickened and for a brief instant it veiled the moon. Michael climbed on his bike and rode up towards Island Road, where he turned, keeping the vast desert of water to his right. He had decided to take his time and ride right through the island, looking, remembering, wondering. By drawing this circle he would make a perfect ending of it.

The ring was still on his finger when Leila woke him up.

'Millie's here,' she said, pushing his bulk with the flat of her hand, 'and we need to take the things out of the bedroom and pack.'

Michael opened his eyes. His wife looked tired even at this early hour of the day. She left him and he dressed slowly. Sleep still scratched in the corner of his eyes and his tongue felt heavy and coated.

He moved into the front room and picked up his son, who was crying loudly and trying to keep the sun out of his face. In the corner of the room the old fan hummed as it turned to face first one wall, then swung back through its motorized curve to face the next. Leila and Millie, their backsides upended, their bodies jacknifed, rummaged noiselessly through the boxes and baskets scattered around their feet like discarded fruit.

'So what happen, you both deaf or what?'

Leila stood and stretched, one hand supporting the base of her spine. She took their child from Michael, sat and pressed his damp mouth to an already erect nipple. Millie turned, her dark face bright.

'So you can't say "morning"?' asked Millie, an eyebrow raised like a question mark.

'Yes, I can say "morning",' said Michael, as he moved past his wife and child towards the open door.

'I have to rush or I going be late.'

'Late for what?' asked Millie. 'The whole day not big enough for the both of you to drink?'

Millie straightened up. Her dress hung crooked, for her shoulders were not wide enough to hold both straps. Michael ignored the question and left. Before starting up the bike he pulled his sunglasses out from the top pocket of his shirt and put them on. He made some minor adjustments so they sat still on his nose. Then he was ready.

Bradeth was pacing the dust outside the Day to Dawn bar.

'What time you call this?'

'Time you put a comb across your head,' said Michael, 'for your hair all bush up like the top of Monkey Hill.' Bradeth sucked his teeth.

'I say what time you call this?'

'I don't know, man.'

'Well, it's time you were here long time is what time it is.'

112

'Hush nuh, man, and buy me a beer. I mean you standing there drinking like you is the only one in the world allowed to work up a thirst.'

'So what happen you forget how to order a beer?'

'I don't forget, I just don't have the money, man. You not going help out a partner?'

'Hush, I already buy a crate and put it inside out of the sun.'

'Well fetch it nuh, man. Then we can sit here and drink, for I feeling like a bottle or two.' Bradeth sucked his teeth again.

He turned and ambled into the bar as Michael took up his seat for the day. Then he staggered out with the crate and let it crash to the ground. He opened a bottle and grinned coyly.

'Michael, you want one?'

'Yes man, I want one.'

'How bad?'

'Bad, bad.'

Bradeth tossed the bottle at him, beer slopping out of the top. 'Well, now you have one.'

Michael drank greedily.

'How it taste?'

'Nice, man,' said Michael. 'Nice.'

The late morning sun streamed into the house. Millie stopped and looked closely at Leila who was perspiring like a canecutter.

'You feeling alright?'

Leila did not answer.

'You should rest up a minute.'

Leila peered over her friend's shoulder and out through the almost permanently open door. Across the road the naked children bathed under the rusty stand-pipe which dribbled water on to their boneless limbs. They splashed and played as best they could. It was already a clear hot day.

'What happen if you get sick on the ship, or boat, or whatever it is you going on?'

113

Leila wiped her forehead.

'I'm just tired, that's all. It'll be alright.'

'It'll be alright,' mimicked Millie. 'It'll be alright when you done kill your arse dead.'

Leila turned and withdrew to the bedroom. Millie sighed deeply, then followed her.

A few minutes later they came back into the front room for a break. There was no need to rush for it would soon be done. Millie poured them some iced water from a pitcher, and Leila looked closely at her. Then Millie caught her friend's eyes, and Leila flushed with embarrassment. She felt she had to say something.

'I'm sure that my mother's going to die by the time we get there. I know it's not a nice thing to say but I'm sure of it.'

'Don't talk so stupid,' said Millie. 'I done tell you already that English medicine is good. There don't going be nothing the matter with she.' Outside a mango dropped to the ground with a dull thud. Neither of them moved. Then Millie continued, 'Anyhow, as far as I'm concerned it's not only your mother's health you got to worry about in England for I hear the white women do anything to get their hands on a piece of coloured man.' Millie paused. 'Don't look so surprised, for I sure you know what I telling you, but that don't be to say that you going have any trouble with Michael. It's just to say that I not prepared to take the risk of that happening between me and Bradeth.'

'So you not planning on ever coming out there?'

Millie sucked her teeth. 'I already done tell you so.'

'But what about Bradeth?'

'What about him? You know I sure he and Michael thinking up some cock and bull plan about all of us going out there together but he must think I stupid.'

'You mean you don't ever want to leave the island?'

Millie raised her voice now. 'It's not a crime, is it? I tell you so on Sunday. I don't have to leave.'

114

'Well, no . . .'

'Then I expect I maybe going come and see you on holiday one time but it's here I belong. You maybe don't see it but me, I love this island with every bone in my body. It's small and poor, and all the rest of the things that you and Michael probably think is wrong with it, but for all of that I still love it. It's my home and home is where you feel a welcome.' She paused. 'Anyhow, I have too much responsibilities to be travelling.'

'The shop?'

'And Shere, and Bradeth, and I soon going be having a next baby.'

Leila's mouth dropped open. 'Millie, when . . . ?'

'About five or six months' time. If it's a boy I call him Bradeth Junior, but if it's another girl I going call she Leila just in case I does never see you again.'

Leila fell into Millie's arms and they hugged each other tightly, like sisters, but in truth they felt closer than that.

Michael ran his forefinger across his close-shaven upper lip and wondered whether or not to grow a moustache. Such a style might be the fashion in England, but then again it might not be. He would just have to wait and see.

Across the road a short, lobster-like man, his gait more shuffle than walk, pushed his wooden box cart of shaved ices down towards the market place, trying to pick up some late afternoon trade. The crippled cart, the two wheels different in size, kicked up a light dust. They watched as he passed out of sight.

Michael's voice rose, his tongue heavy with drink. 'I bet you never coming to England.' He spat into the gutter, then tucked one leg clumsily under the other.

'I coming, you just hold on and see, man.'

Bradeth laughed but his eyes were unmoving. Michael looked at him and noticed, then they were quiet. He would miss Bradeth, perhaps more than he had realized.

They finished their drinks and tossed both bottles on to the already well-established pile of empties. They clattered against each other in a drunken duet.

'You want a next bottle?' asked Bradeth, gesturing to an empty crate. He tried hard not to smile, but his face was alive with mischief. Michael sucked his teeth in fake annoyance.

Bradeth stood, flicked a mosquito from his face, then rocked forward on to the balls of his feet. No matter what time of day it was his body always seemed larger than his shadow. He went into the bar, dragged another crate out into the street and together they slowly drank their way through it. Then they slept, and the drink hummed wildly in their blood, and the occasional car slipped respectfully by.

Bradeth woke with a jolt, a chill slithering through his body. He peered incredulously down the street like a man unsure of his fate.

'What time it is?'

'About time you stopped asking that question,' said Michael, his arms folded, his eyes closed.

'Look, man, I'm serious,' said Bradeth, trying to get to his feet. 'It's darkness already, so we better be getting along.' Michael opened his eyes and rubbed some life into them.

'Maybe you talking right for once,' he said, as he re-assembled his crumpled body using Bradeth's arm to lever himself upright. They stood together, the only two figures in view, and they looked aimlessly about themselves.

'Well, then, we going on your bike?'

Michael licked a finger, bent over and started to rub some dirt from his trouser knee.

'What bike?' he asked, almost losing his balance as he rubbed vigorously.

'What you mean "what bike?" Your arse must be really drunk, boy, for it's your bike I see standing over there or you blind or what?'

Michael walked over to it, looked, then walked back to his friend.

116

'Your head mash up?' asked Bradeth. Michael laughed.

'It don't look like my bike to me,' he said, digging his hands into his trouser pocket. He pulled out two keys on a plain silver ring and forced them into Bradeth's hand. 'Look like your bike to me.'

Bradeth stared back and forth from his open palm, the keys sitting neatly in its centre, to the bike, and back again to his palm. Then he turned and looked at Michael.

'You mean it?'

'Course I mean it. I don't joke about your bike. We can walk down there and you can pick it up later.'

Michael slipped his arm around Bradeth's shoulder and they began to trip gently in the general direction of the harbour. Behind them hobbled a stray dog, its feet blistered by the heat of the day, its head low with exhaustion. Michael laughed hard and pulled his friend close. Bradeth doubled his laughter and they veered crazily down the road towards England.

As they neared the harbour and the hour of midnight, they heard late voices in a side street, then the hollow thud of a soft ball hitting an oil-drum wicket. The young boys whooped and hollered, then argued, then accepted the decision of the invisible umpire, democracy. The next man in, a stick-like boy in stained shorts, otherwise naked apart from the heat and dust of the day, scratched a crease into the earth with his hopeless bat.

ENGLAND

Outside a thick mist wrapped itself around the street. Leila bit her bottom lip and trembled like a needle on a gauge. She took the long curve and walked with head bent, shoulders sloping, towards the bus stop. She clung to a small cluster of bright flowers. As she passed by, the children stopped playing, seemingly more out of habit than curiosity. She remembered that this was a school holiday and they had nothing else to do while their parents were at work. At the end of the street she joined a short queue of six or seven people, all of them West Indians, and waited for the bus. Across the road a lorry hurtled by, throwing up bits of rubbish and paper high in the air.

She sat in the front seat on the top deck of the bus, looking down at the people and the life in the street below. She noticed that in some areas there were many coloured people and in other areas there were very few. She noticed that coloured people did not drive big cars or wear suits or carry briefcases, that they seemed to look sad and cold. She noticed that the eyes of the white people on the posters never left her no matter how quickly she glanced at them. The rivers that the bus lurched over were like dirty brown lines, full of empty bottles and cigarette ends, cardboard boxes and greying suds of pollution. Leila knew that this was normal. She would have to try harder to get used to such things if she was going to make anything of her life here.

The bus turned another corner and Leila stared out of the window. She worried about her mother, whom she was going to visit. She looked at the snaking, endless streets which were full of people carrying umbrellas, weaving in and out of one another's paths, so hurried, private English faces with newspapers and rubbish curled around their feet like dead vines. Then the bus splashed to a halt at a new set of traffic lights, and Leila noticed that the lettering got smaller and more hurried, as if the artist was running out of paint and time.

'IF YOU WANT A NIGGER NEIGHBOUR VOTE LABOUR.'

They turned right into a road where the children played happily among broken bottles and bricks. Between the identical houses she could see not even the smallest fraction of an inch. Then the bus stopped to wait for a lorry to pull out and Leila looked down a side street. Two little girls, their faces blackened with grime and filth, bounced merrily upon an old mattress. For a moment they forgot their other friends and lost themselves in simple pleasure.

On the street corner a middle-aged woman, painted to appear as if young, modelled with a lamp-post. She looked dirty. Leila thought she probably smelled even worse. A child, a coloured boy, who needed a good bath and a meal, stared at the bus and wiped his nose across the back of his sleeve. This is not yet winter, thought Leila, and the boy has a cold. The bus moved off and passed another of the women, this one leaning up against a parked car and filing her nails, happy to leave the lamp-posts vacant. Leila looked away and began to try and calculate the number of times she had made this journey to the hospital.

It was four months since she first made the journey. On that day she had followed Michael down the steps, off the bus and just the few paces into the etherized sterility of the hospital foyer which greeted them with a determined blast of hot air. Neither of them had quite known where they were. Leila had felt anxious as she looked around at the clean floors and walls. The patients who wandered or waited in the corridors looked to her like discarded tailor's dummies. Michael would not meet her eyes. He seemed unconcerned, so she took Calvin from him in order to comfort herself.

'It must be down here,' he said, as if Leila were stupid not to know her way around this English hospital.

As they marched smoothly through the corridors their shoes echoed. The journey seemed endless, but eventually they stopped in front of a pair of solid doors, each punctuated by a small round window. A young nurse with sloppy hips and a crooked smile paddled towards them. She ushered them through the doors and into the ward as if she knew exactly who it was they had come to visit.

Leila's mother had large flashes of grey in her hair. Though her eyes were closed it was clear that she was not sleeping. Leila sat on the bed and pulled her mother's arms out from underneath the sheet. She held both her cold hands in hers. Her mother opened her eyes but she said nothing. She closed them again as if not sure who it was she was looking at. Then Leila began to cry and Michael stepped forward and placed his arm dutifully around his wife's shoulders. Leila said nothing. He made a quick gesture towards the door with his head but she ignored him. Eventually Michael lowered his mouth to his wife's ear and told her he would soon be back.

'I'm going for a walk,' he said, almost as an afterthought.

Like a child awakening from a deep sleep Leila's mother stretched, then curled up again, then opened her eyes and looked all about her as if making sure of where she was. She propped herself up as best she could and began talking to her daughter as if a long conversation had been interrupted by a discreet trip to the lavatory.

'So you finding England cold?' Her voice was slow, more tired than unhurried.

'I think I'll survive,' said Leila, her face widening into a smile.

'Good.' Her mother paused. 'And how is your husband?'

'Things are fine,' said Leila.

Her mother laughed quietly.

'You don't change at all, do you? Still the diplomat.' She paused, this time to catch her breath. 'Who call the boy Calvin?' She felt her grandson's cheek with the back of her hand.

'I did,' said Leila nervously.

'It's a nice name. A nice name for the boy.' They both looked at Calvin, then Leila spoke.

'How are you feeling these days?'

'I'm feeling alright. A little tired but I can't complain.'

Every time her mother breathed there was a high asthmatic whistle. Leila knew she was lying.

'Did they say when you can come out?'

Her mother smiled. 'Soon, not long now.' Again she had lied.

'Well, when you do you must come and live with us. We're going to look for a place big enough for all of us.'

Her mother managed a small laugh. Then she squeezed her daughter's hand.

'Leila, child, London is not my home.'

Leila looked away but her mother continued to stare at her.

'And I don't want you to forget that either.'

Leila fought back the tears in her eyes. She had always felt a child could never understand the illogicality of a parent's love until the child was a parent itself. But sadly, though Leila now felt she understood her mother a little better, her mother did not seem to have changed in her feelings towards her. That she loved her she did not doubt, but, as always, Leila wished there was something more, something that would make her mother more like a friend. As it was they just sat and stared at each other. The pain of illness, the pain of marriage, the pain of a journey across the world and the happiness of a small baby for them both to share, nothing seemed to be able to bring them together and this first exchange had been more interview than conversation.

Colonial raping the island

But Leila was not to know that her mother had never wanted a child. In fact she had never wanted a man, for when she saw her first penis hanging with arrogance before her, its owner at least fifty years older than her, a great-uncle, she knew deep in her heart that the coupling of man and woman would hold no fascination for her.

Eventually, as the old man conjured a stiffness into himself and climbed on her, grunting loudly as he did so, all she could think of was that as long as he did not die on top of her she promised herself and God that she would go to church every Sunday. But luckily, almost as soon as he had forced his way into her body, all the tension rushed from his loins and, too old to be embarrassed, he simply climbed down, wiped himself off on the loose tail of his shirt, and left 10 cents by the gas lamp for her to buy some ice cream.

And every week he managed to drag Leila's mother into his house on the pretext of some errand, and every week she would rearrange her clothes and pick up her ten cents and skip past him out into the street as if nothing had happened, although she was as yet too young to know that older eyes followed her and knew differently. But then he died, not on top of her as she had always feared, but of a final and sudden bronchial attack as he prepared to unbutton his trousers. Leila's mother was able to run out into the street and scream, knowing full well that he was fully clothed and nothing had taken place. And of course everybody felt sorry for her, as she hoped they would, but the main thing was that his penis was hidden, that was all she could think about. He did not die with his penis hanging out.

There followed a swift volley of lovers who taught Leila's mother what it felt like to be kissed on the toes and the fingers, who taught her what it felt like to have a man's mouth around her breast and his fingers snaking in and out of the cracks in her body. But after they had gone she always felt used, like a canvas upon which an artist has toyed in light pencil. She felt as though her lovers were playing; that they gained their real satisfaction elsewhere.

But then, as the final man sliced into her body, a young man of almost her own age, she was overcome with the horror of the fact that in less than six months' time her first child, not his child, a child that belonged to all of them and none of them, would be breaking its way out of her body. In her panic she came timidly, just once, but her man's penis did not notice and his body raced on as if late for the inter-island boat.

Leila was born the day war was declared in Europe; there was no real significance in this, except Leila's mother might have forgotten the day of her birth had it not been celebrated elsewhere for different reasons. She was too small, very light, and she did not cry. These were the only three things her mother could remember about her. Of her feelings about herself that day she remembered much more, especially the pain. She had looked down and seen the beach-ball of a head, far too large for her body, and realized that the child was making a cave of her vagina.

But as Leila grew up her mother learned to love her more each day, not because she would be her only child, not even because she was her constant and only companion, but because of Leila's sharp intelligence, which always made her think twice as quickly as any adult had ever made her. It was as if Leila had shot some urgency and direction back into her life. The three men from whom she demanded money, accusing them all of being the father and threatening to expose them as molesters if they even so much as looked at Leila, these white men eyed their daughter from afar and happily paid the money safe in the knowledge that they had a real relationship with the island that would live on after they left. Leila's mother barely spoke to them: she took their money and put it in the bank. She hoped that she would have no need to spend it so that her daughter might one day have it. And the day she pulled Leila towards her and hoisted the child's bare foot into her lap, so that her daughter lost her balance and had to grab on to her, this was the day, thank the Lord, she knew she had successfully completed the first part of her task. In the years to come her daughter would thank her for this, more than she would the money.

She pulled the white sock over Leila's toes and unrolled it, tube-like, up the full length of her skinny leg. Then she did the same with the other sock and turned her daughter around so that she could take a good look at her. The previous night she had slept very little, worried as to whether she should walk with Leila to the edge of the road and wait for her to catch the school bus with the other children, or whether she should, on this her first day, let her go on her own. She stared at the back of her daughter's head, wondering if the child could tell what her mother was thinking. She knew children, especially bright children like Leila, possessed an unknown power feared by most adults. Then her child slipped her grip and turned around to face her, with eyes large and searching. In the distance they both heard the bus.

'You better go now,' said her mother, 'and look after yourself.'

Leila felt as though her mother were about to push her under a car. She stood in disbelief, not understanding why she was not coming with her.

'Leila, you didn't hear what I said, girl? Go.'

Her mother's words sounded as though they had been placed in her mouth by another person, and Leila was sure it was a game. It was only this that prevented her from crying. But, though she did not cry, she also chose not to leave the house, and her mother eventually had no choice but to raise her hand and beat her until she left.

It was many years before her mother would beat her again, for the second and only other time. As with the first beating Leila did not understand why it was she was being punished. Her mother had stood above her on the beach and reached down and slapped her hard across the face. Then they had walked home together, Leila in front, her mother two steps behind. When they reached St Patrick's her mother made her shower in the street, under the rusty stand-pipe, naked and fourteen. The tears that lined her face outnumbered the thin streams of water that arched around her shoulders and down her back. Some of the children were still playing but they did not laugh, they just watched. Leila felt that this was worse than if they had laughed. They formed a loose semi-circle and witnessed an emotional execution.

All she had done was go and lie down beside the people and see what it was like. They were friendly, or at least the man was, the woman was asleep, or pretending to be asleep. He passed over some of the sweet-smelling oil for her to rub all over her body. She still had on her school uniform so he encouraged her to take off the tie and hoist up her skirt a little. Perhaps she should undo the first few buttons on her blouse. After all, it's the skin that we want to burn, not the clothes. Leila had laughed and kicked off her shoes. She wiped what remained of the oil into her hands, but it would not go away, so she wiped it on the outside of her schoolbag. Then she lay back with her two friends, her hands behind her head, and looked up as directly into the sun as she dared. The man asked her name, and where she was from, and where she went to school, but the woman said nothing. He never told Leila anything about himself, but Leila did not ask. She preferred to sink into the silences rather than try and blot them out with her own childish voice. Then one silence fell deeper than the rest, and Leila realized that he, like his wife or girlfriend, had tumbled into sleep and she lay alone, smelling odd and feeling rather foolish. Then her mother obscured the sun and the day exploded in Leila's face.

In the morning Leila had prepared herself for school, dreading the moment she would have to leave her room and take breakfast. When she appeared her mother greeted her as normal and pretended that nothing had happened, but this only served to make Leila feel more nervous. Then, as she picked up her bag ready to leave, she smelled the oil she had wiped on it and the odour nearly made her vomit. Her mother gently touched the side of Leila's face with her hand, and kissed her on the forehead. As Leila turned to go she held her back.

'Don't never let me catch you lying with white people again or as God's my witness I'll take a stick to you and beat you till the life leaves your body.'

Leila stared at her, but this only spurred her mother on further.

'You think you can trust them? You can't. And if you think the white woman was sleeping you were wrong. White women never sleep with both eyes closed if a coloured woman is around, and they never see a coloured man without something moving inside of them. Still, you going live to find that out.'

The bus passed a third woman, this one by a lamp-post, then stopped. After the bell had rung out it started again. Leila stood up, pleased that her journey would soon be at an end. She was ambivalent about the value of these daily visits to her mother. Nearly every day for four months, Sundays apart, Leila had finally calculated that this must be her 106th visit and still neither their conversation nor her mother's health improved. Even before she got to the hospital the endless views of decay and poverty only made her feel more depressed. She often wondered why London Transport did not put dark glass in the windows of the buses on some routes, like the glass she saw in ambulances. Her route to the hospital was one of those that would benefit.

The nurse was waiting outside the ward for Leila to appear. For the first ten minutes the doctor had waited with her, but he had to go and attend to some of the other patients. The nurse tried to remain calm but she moved nervously, as though she needed to use the toilet.

Leila walked toward her, holding her small cluster of bright flowers.

'Getting colder,' began Leila.

The nurse smiled, but Leila could see. She pushed past the woman and ran the full length of the ward. She stopped at her mother's bedside, as if momentarily unsure, then she pressed the flowers up to her face. The bed was empty, the new sheets still folded, the mattress exposed. On this her 106th visit to the hospital her mother had died. The previous day she must have been dying. Leila felt stricken with guilt that she had not acted upon what she had seen.

Her mother had managed to smile but she had been disturbed in her mind. In her body she had been more frail than drowsy.

'Michael beat you yet, girl?' she had asked, as if asking for a glass of water.

Leila had almost let go of her hand, but her mother grabbed at it and tried to crush it.

'He beating you?'

'No,' said Leila, her surprise impossible to disguise.

'Well, don't sound so shocked, for I'm sure you realize that men beat women. But no man ever beat me.' She paused, then went on.

'Once a man get so mad with me over some fruit he said I stole that he chase me through the whole length of the village. It was a hot day, not like today, and you could hear pan beating for miles. Eventually I fall over and I can't run no more, I looked up and he's standing over me as if to say, 'I've got you now so don't run.' But I can't run no more anyhow so he didn't have nothing to worry about. Then he tried to beat me with a long piece of cane but I didn't cry out or nothing. I just got up, though I don't know where I found the strength, and I took the stick and I broke it in half, you hear me?' Leila nodded.

130

'And then I had to walk back on my own and it's the longest walk I ever made, past Frances Gumb's place, round the bend and into the village where everyone is standing and staring at me, all of them thinking how he must have beat me bad. Me, I just kept my head high, girl, and I walked on till I heard somebody laugh and then a next person crack out and suddenly everybody is laughing at me and I start to feel the water in my eyes but I can't run away. So I just kept walking and I know that no man is ever going to beat me, for it's not the licks that hurt, it's the people that know about it, and are letting you know they know, even though they don't know a damn thing.'

Yesterday Leila had smiled weakly, as if it was nothing to do with her, a good story well told, and her mother had smiled back at her in a different fashion. Then she closed her eyes, slowly, as if drawing long curtains in an already darkened room.

The doctor touched Leila's arm.

'It's alright, Mrs Preston.'

He spoke with the studied concern of a professional. Leila pushed the flowers hard into her face and she stared at the empty bed. Then she smelled the doctor's breath. It did not smell good. It smelled stale, and his voice sounded hard, like heavy feet on gravel. Her forty-one-year-old mother was dead, and she looked up into his face, wanting to see if his mind was panicking or if this was just another skilled part of a skilled job.

Leila pulled away from him as he began to talk about the funeral arrangements. She felt sorry for him. He shrugged his apologetic shoulders and nervously tapped his fountain pen against his wrist-watch. She left the hospital and walked out into the cold afternoon air, still holding the crushed flowers. She drifted away from everybody; it made no sense.

Five, maybe six stops from home, Leila leaped up and pushed her way to the back of the bus and down the stairs. She jumped off and began to jostle her way through the busy pedestrians. Then she ran, as fast as she could, and grabbed the woman by the shoulders and spun her around; then she fell down and began to sob. People stopped and looked, but the woman simply leaned forward and stretched out her hand to help her. Leila looked up at her. It was not her mother, but the coloured woman whose hand she took looked like she too was going to cry.

Unable to speak with anyone, Leila decided to walk back in the rain. To have asked for a bus ticket would have been too much. Though she knew the way, it was getting dark. Leila slitted her eyes so that all she could see were the wipers of the passing cars slashing back and forth through the pounding rain, and their lights reflecting in the puddles. She lowered her head and walked, but eventually she could walk no further. On the other side of the road was a small church, but strung out between her and the church door were line upon line of cars. Leila waited and shivered in the rain. When the line broke she dashed across the road and pushed at the heavy oak. It creaked open and she shut it behind her.

Inside was silent and almost totally still, dark but candlelit. Leila crossed herself and walked down the centre aisle, past the straight, tortured benches, towards the organ pipes. She knelt in the front pew, bowed her head and prayed hard, clasping her hands tightly together as if trying to squeeze out the rain water from between her sodden palms. Why? Her mother had done nobody any wrong. She had done nobody any harm. She had come to England. She had tried. Didn't these people understand? Didn't they understand that she barely knew her mother, that everything up until now had been a preparation for knowing, not the knowing itself. Her mother was almost a stranger, and even after four months in England Leila had never given up hope that she might still get to know her. Finally, Leila had no words except 'please'.

The priest stood in the darkness at the back of the church. He watched her. Then he sat. He listened to her uttering her one word over and over again, and he wanted to come up and put a hand on her shoulder, but she was just a child. He knew she would get over it, whatever it was.

The young English girl from next door was trying to feed Calvin when a swollen-eyed Leila arrived home.

'Are you alright?' she asked.

Leila managed a smile. She took Calvin from her and looked into his face. He was not hungry, but the girl was not to know.

'Michael hasn't been back so I suppose he must be at work still.' Leila did not answer so the girl got up to leave.

'It's getting late so I'd best be on my way. My mum's been round twice wondering where you'd got to and she said if you weren't back by ten she'd phone the hospital.'

The girl was leaving when Leila spoke up. 'I'll see her tomorrow.'

The girl stared at Leila. 'Alright?'

'Alright,' confirmed Leila under her breath. 'Alright.'

Leila sat heavily and looked at Calvin. Then she heard the girl slam the front door and she remembered her friend's voice.

'For it's when a man don't even call his child by its own name that you got problems, you hear me. When he starts to call the child, "it", or "that", or "thing", then I going start to worry about how Bradeth feeling about me, till then I not too worried for if I say he going marry to me then I don't care what my Aunt Toosie say, he going marry to me.'

From the direction of her mother's bedroom they had both heard a low firing of coughs. Millie had looked anxiously at Leila, who had shrugged her shoulders as if helpless to do anything.

'You think Michael going want to marry to you?' asked Millie.

Leila spoke quietly, not wanting to disturb her mother.

'I don't know.'

'Don't know, my arse. You don't think about nothing else all day long, and you treat him like it's him alone can make the sun go up in the morning and the moon come out at night.'

'No, I don't.'

'Don't what!' interrupted Millie. 'Your mother have you living like a princess all your life and as soon as she get sick you gone wild: first Arthur, then Michael, you think people don't talk? Well?'

Leila picked up Calvin and slowly made her way upstairs. She opened the door to the bedroom which these days was like opening the door to a fridge. Tonight she did not notice. She undressed in the dark and climbed into bed alone. Where Michael was and what he might be doing did not concern her; he had told her this many times, but tonight she felt it in herself. Leila leaned over and lifted Calvin from his cot. She took him into the bed with her. He, like her, lay on his back and stared at the ceiling. She, like him, chose not to cry. Not tonight.

THE PASSAGE

On the fifteenth day the wind died and Leila saw land; the high and irregular cliffs of England through the cold grey mist of the English channel. She clasped together the collar of her light cotton dress and shivered. Overhead a thin fleet of clouds cast a bleak shadow across the deck, and the sluggish water swelled gently, then slackened. Leila stood at the front of the ship with six or seven more. Nobody spoke. It was still early and they waited, as if trapped in a glass case, while the other voyagers were still getting up, or feeling sick, or sleeping.

The thin white strip of cliff grew vertically as an hour passed and the ship edged its way towards land. Then the word spread and the group multiplied to a crowd and Leila felt herself being pushed.

She turned and walked away towards the rear of the ship, stepping over luggage and prostrate bodies as she did so. It was like a Saturday market on deck, for some had dashed up to see England, though still tired. As they could not be bothered to go back downstairs they simply lay down where they had stood, and they now dozed. The funnels above continued to cough smoke; Leila leaned over the railings and looked at the sea bursting into foam in the ship's wake. She realized just how far they had come and felt thankful it would not be long now, even though her heart felt heavy and apprehensive, fearful that she had been reading too much hope into her mother's letters. Unable to share her distress with anyone, she had therefore lived out this passage in more mental than physical discomfort, knowing the world she had left behind no longer held anything of interest for her save Millie and Bradeth. The world she was choosing to inhabit might hold even less if she could not share it fully with her mother. She straightened up and looked out at the sea. She began to hum idly, trying to drain her mind.

After a few minutes Leila felt cold so she left the deck and made her way down the narrow, dimly lit staircase. At the bottom of the steps she walked along the iron rectangle which was the corridor, and at the end of it she passed into the cabin which had been her home for the last two weeks. Michael lay asleep, as he had done for most of the journey, but now his face seemed to have lost its feverish pallor. He appeared to be dreaming peaceably, rather than hallucinating or fighting off illness, and his feet stared out brazenly from beneath the bottom of the grey blanket. Leila shut the door.

The noises in the cabin disturbed her, but it was only the dull rumble of the engine and the loose hum of the glass in the porthole. She covered Michael's feet before reaching up to the top bunk and retrieving Calvin. Then she peeled back the thin straps from her shoulders and exposed an oversized nipple. Her son had to be fed; she did not know when she would get another chance. As she held him up to her breast she squatted slightly so she could look out of the porthole.

Calvin did not want any more milk. She patted her son on the back, encouraging him to belch. Michael woke up. He watched, as if he had never witnessed such behaviour, then he swung himself out of bed and stooped down beside her. He looked long and hard but said nothing. Leila did not ask him what he was thinking. She laid Calvin back on the top bunk and started to pack their things. Michael, who was dressed only in shorts and vest, stood up and unhooked his clothes from behind the door. The cabin was so small he barely needed to move to reach them. As they prepared themselves in silence Leila sighed.

Most of the journey had been spent nursing husband and son, continually fetching food from the kitchens, bringing Michael a small tin bowl in which to wash, assisting him in his frequent journeys to the toilet, washing Calvin's clothes and then having to sit up on deck with the damp washing as the cold wind whipped through the ship. She was frightened to leave the washing in case anyone tried to walk off with the nappies; for two weeks it had been a full-time job. It was often late at night by the time both husband and son finally fell asleep, and it was only then that she had some time to herself.

Usually she would go back out on deck and think of her mother, whom she hoped would be well enough to meet them. But it was at this point that her thoughts became too painful and she tried to make her mind stop working. She would look around at the sad brown gazes of her fellow emigrants, men and women who lined up before her like the cast of some tragic opera. There was the old man who sat as if close to tears, his large jocular chin glued to the palm of his hand, his crooked elbow to his knee, his eyes staring out into the distance as if unable to reconcile the conflict of where he had come from with where he was going to. A little to his left lay slumped the woman with the wicker baskets, her hair scraped up on top of her head as if with the sharp edge of a trowel, her dress so short that it rode up over her swollen black frame every time she moved. When she laughed the flabby tops of her thighs were totally exposed and some still turned to look, though, by now thoroughly familiar with the scene, they merely wondered what it was she laughed at. And the drunk occupied the canvas chair. He never left it and he never smiled. The bristles on his face looked so hard that Leila imagined you would cut your hand if you were brave enough to go across and touch him. They were flecked, like guano in colour, and beside him lay the empty rum bottle that would soon, and mysteriously, be replaced by a full one. This deck looked like a slum street, the suitcases houses, and Leila would turn away and stare at the white spits of foam in the distance in order not to get too depressed.

It was nearly 12 now and she had finished packing. Their one suitcase lay on the bottom bunk. For some inexplicable reason there seemed to be more to get into the case than there had been when she and Millie had packed it two weeks earlier. It puzzled her. Calvin, now freshly changed and washed, lay gurgling to himself.

Then Michael came back. He had been up on deck with the rest of the passengers, their jackets, skirts, dresses, ties, all rippling in the stiff but friendly breeze.

'You ready?' he asked, all signs of his previous illness having vanished. Leila nodded and picked up Calvin as Michael reached for the suitcase.

'People up there queuing to get off the boat already so we better take up a place.'

Michael left the room without looking backwards, but Leila stood for a moment and thought. She had grown attached to this coffin-like cabin, for it was a final reminder of home. She broke it, knowing that any weakness now could only be bad preparation for what might follow.

On deck Michael had already struck up conversation with a group of men, three of them in panama hats and double-breasted suits, the fourth in trilby and blazer and Oxford bags. As Leila listened their conversation became loud, fast, furious and exclusive.

'Me? Know anything about England? Look man, I been reading about the place since I five.'

'So what you been reading?'

'Yes, man, what books you read? You read *History of the English People* by Winston Churchill?'

'I read that one.'

'Me an' all.'

'Yes, man, I sure everybody read it. It's a standard.'

'A classic.'

'It's a classic too but I wants to know if you does read it as yet.'

'Twice.'

'Twice what, my arse?'

'Twice straight through but if it's a text you looking for you should read *Encyclopedia Britannica*.'

'Which volume?'

'All of them.'

'I read them.'

'All of them?'

'Sure, man.'

'Me an' all.'

'So what it do tell you about England?'

'Everything.'

'And more.'

'Much more.'

'Industrial Revolution.'

'It's right. It's a big thing in England, man. I can see you is a scholar for true.'

'I tell you it's a classic text as well. Churchill don't be nobody's fool, boy.'

'So who lead it, then?'

'What you mean who lead it? It's not fucking Russian revolution we talking about.'

'I know that, man, but I mean who is in charge of it.'

'You hear him, you hear him! He wants to know who is in charge of the Industrial Revolution.'

'Well, somebody must be in charge if it's that big.'

'You talking shit, boy.'

'Why?'

'Coz it's shit talk.'

'I think the king lead it.'

'But it's not the same thing.'

'Anyway, if I does remember my history lessons right it's a queen ruling then.'

'So it's queen who leading the revolution?'

'If you like.'

'So where you study history lessons, man?'

'London University external student.'

'Well, no wonder you know so much about it, then.'

'Yes, man, no wonder. You must come half-English already.'

'Me arse.'

Leila listened to them, but she watched the drama unfolding around her. The crew in their blue woollen hats were preparing to dock. On the decks of the smaller boats the owners took a break from their summer repairs. They stood up and watched as the emigrant ship slid smoothly past the beacons, the sea wall and the lighthouse. Then the ship's engines were cut, almost as a mark of respect, and Leila watched as they took their place among the cranes and cargo. A colony of white faces stared up at them. The men finished their conversation.

'Me, I don't never see so many white people in my life.'

'Well, I suppose they don't ever see so many coloured people either.'

'It's true,' said a wise man, 'but we all the same flag, the same empire'.

For the first time in two weeks the ship shuddered to a halt.

Leila looked at England, but everything seemed bleak. She quickly realized she would have to learn a new word; overcast. There were no green mountains, there were no colourful women with baskets on their heads selling peanuts or bananas or mangoes, there were no trees, no white houses on the hills, no hills, no wooden houses by the shoreline, and the sea was not blue and there was no beach, and there were no clouds, just one big cloud, and they had arrived.

The walkway was pushed into place and jammed up against the side of the ship. Gathering up their luggage, they began, one by one, to disembark in front of the television and newsreel cameras. Leila watched as she participated. A windswept plank down to the shore, somebody's hat blowing away, babies wrapped up like Christmas gifts and clinging

142

desperately to mothers, women with dark mournful eyes, headscarves and petticoats of fiery pink peering out from beneath their knee-length dresses; more men in panama hats and leather trilbys, some in colourful sleeveless sweaters, white shirts, handkerchiefs large and clean and prominent. She followed Michael, and the man in front of them knelt and kissed the ground. They both stepped around him and followed the rest of the passengers into the customs hall.

Like everybody else, they had nothing to declare except their accents. Leila dug deep in her bag and pulled clear their joint British passport. It was brand new. It was stamped in silence, the customs officer just glancing up once to make sure the faces in the passport matched those standing before him. Then they passed out into the next hall where relatives and friends were gathered. They were all coloured. The white people on the quayside must have been local people just watching. Still, thought Leila, it was the same back home when a big ship came in.

They moved through this hall and followed a sign which said, 'Trains'. Leila searched for their rail vouchers while Michael looked up ahead. There was a gate, and slowly they began to move towards it as the noise of escaping steam grew louder and more frightening. Calvin began to cry. It was as if, hidden away and out of sight, some huge snarling monster was about to pounce, but Leila comforted him and he stopped crying. When they reached the gate Michael took the vouchers from his wife and passed them to the man, who pointed unnecessarily towards the solitary train.

Leila gazed through the cold window of the train. She watched as her warm breath misted up the glass. The fields had little in them save a few sheep here and there. Some cows stood silent and still, like statues. Where was the food they grew to feed themselves? As they plunged further inland, she wondered how it was that people managed to live so far away from the sea. Leila looked across at Michael, but he was already fast asleep. She turned her attention back to the window. Then, just as she was acclimatizing herself to the tall electricity pylons which spoiled the view, the train plunged into a black tunnel. Then a thick road cut along the fringes of the fields. The cars, tens of them, rushed madly along, all different colours and different sizes. Then the chimneys began to multiply, and the greenness disappeared, and they were in a town, and Leila could no longer keep her eyes open.

When she awoke she could see that they must have passed through the town, but the new fields seemed bigger and less shapely. She could sense too that soon the chimneys would be upon them again. Outside it began to rain. It was a sort of half-rain which left whole drops of water compressed against the window. Leila watched them silently running into each other. A few minutes later the world turned grey and black, the sky took on an ashen hue, and Leila thought it looked like a hurricane was going to blow up. Again she glanced across at Michael but he seemed calm, as did Calvin, whom she held in her arms. They both, father and son, dozed lightly and peacefully.

The houses and the streets and the cars seemed to be going on for ever. The huge jug-shaped towers, and the great posters advertising coffee and cereal and cigarettes, and the broken, crumbling lips of the chimneys, all of this caught Leila's eyes. Already she was used to the red double decker buses, but she worried slightly for she could see no end to this town which fought off freedom of the fields and the low hills. Then the train began to slow down. It jolted to a halt and Michael woke up. Leila looked through the window at the sign which read, 'Victoria Station'. She knew now they were in London.

Michael pulled down their case from the rack and opened the sliding door. The passengers in the corridor were moving past, single file, seemingly reluctant to let them out. Eventually the train emptied and they could move.

Leila stepped down on to the platform, but it was like stepping into a spacious black room for there was a ceiling and birds circled overhead. There were other trains too, neatly arranged in parallel lines, blowing off steam like long distance runners catching their breath after a hard race. Michael joined his wife.

As they approached the front of the train they began to bunch up together as if preparing to enter the narrow end of a funnel. One by one they squeezed through and found themselves in a large pen bounded by makeshift wooden fencing. Behind the fencing were rows of spectators. The emigrants stood silently and shouted with their eyes for their friends and families. Michael put down the suitcase while the English people looked on. He listened, fascinated, as up above a huge voice continually boomed out, talking about the trains, and the platforms from which they would be leaving, and the times at which they would be leaving, and the times at which they would be arriving.

A woman in a Salvation Army uniform came towards Leila and offered her a cup of soup. But Leila looked away, so the woman gave the soup to an old man; she watched over him as he drank it. Leila looked for her mother but could not see her. It was useless. And the truth was she did not now expect to find her among these English people, so she moved away.

After the black interior of the station the sharp daylight caught Leila by surprise. It was not a particularly bright day, but at least she felt able to breathe freely again. Once outside she looked at her mother's address while Michael looked at the cars and the traffic.

'Which way is it to the address?' Michael managed to ask the question without seeming in the slightest bit interested. Leila looked at him as if ready to give up now.

'I don't know, Michael. I've never been to England before.'

'Then maybe we better take a taxi.'

The square black taxis came about one every two minutes, and soon there was only a tall Englishman ahead of them. A taxi came and the man climbed in without glancing back. Then, as the taxi swished away, another one arrived. The driver rolled down his window.

'Where to, guv?'

Michael read the scrap of paper with the address on it, then he stood half-questioning the existence of such a place. He offered the piece of paper to the driver.

'Can't you pronounce this?' asked the driver. 'Quaxley Street.' He leaned back and opened the door for them with his trailing hand.

'Well, come on then, unless you want to stand out in the rain all day.'

The door had opened the wrong way. Leila bent down, carried Calvin in and sat at the far side. Michael eased his way into the back beside her and the driver slammed the door shut.

Eventually he spoke again. 'That'll be £2 10 shillings, guv.'

Leila gave the man a £5 note. She checked the change carefully, folded it and put it away in her bag. She did not fully understand the sarcasm of his 'Well, thanks a lot, missus', but she did not care.

From the outside the house looked thin and flat, as did all the other houses on the street. It had two small steps up to the door and it stood three storeys high.

'All this house can't belong to your mother,' began Michael.

'I don't know,' was Leila's reply.

A small group of coloured children gathered in the street. Leila turned and smiled at them, coyly at first, then more confidently when they smiled back at her.

'I going sound this bell and see what happens.' Michael pressed the bell and waited. Nothing happened.

'You think I should sound the next one?'

Leila jogged Calvin up and down in her arms, trying to keep both of them warm.

'Sound it, then.'

Michael pressed it, then stood back. Almost instantly a window on the second floor flew open and an irate head snaked out.

'What the hell it is you all want?'

The head belonged to a coloured man who seemed a very tired thirty.

'We've come to see Mrs Franks,' shouted Michael. 'We've just arrived from home.' *Paradol ?*

The man looked down at them, his eyes narrowed against the afternoon light, and he continued to speak aggressively.

'So wait. You think that because you just get off the boat you can wake me up?'

'What we want to know is if Mrs Franks lives here. My wife here is her daughter.'

'So what you want me to do about it?'

Michael looked at Leila, then back at the man. After a long pause the man relented.

'Okay, I'm coming down.'

The window slammed shut and Michael turned to his wife.

'At least we know she lives here.'

Leila could not answer.

The badly hung door almost fell open, and the man stood before them in striped pyjamas. The children began to laugh and point. His feet, like his hands, were bare and rough, as if lightly brushed with chalk.

'Look, I'm tired, so if you want to come in then come.'

He turned and led the way up the dimly lit stairway.

'We keep going on,' said the man as they began to go up another set of steps. Leila's eyes grew accustomed to the dark.

'In here,' he said, opening a small door and stepping back to allow them to pass into a hallway crammed tightly with newspapers and unwashed clothing. Leila could immediately tell that no woman lived here. He pushed the door shut and pointed with a jerk of his thumb towards another door.

'People asleep in this room here. Over there is the kitchen.'

Leila could see a small room. It had no door. In it was just a cooker and some huge pans.

'Over there is the bathroom, and that door there used to be Mrs Franks's own room but Earl staying there at present. You can wait in there for him but I know he did go to meet you. Make yourself at home for I have to sleep now.'

The man spoke quickly and yawned as he did so. As he turned to go, Leila stepped forward.

'Who's Earl?'

'Earl?' said the man beginning to yawn again. 'Earl?'

'And what about my mother? Where is she?'

'Well, Mrs Franks back in the hospital for test or something.' He saw Leila's face drop. 'But I don't think it's serious. And Earl is the chap who owns the place and who does the collecting up of the rents.'

'What hospital?' asked Leila.

'I don't know,' he said, eager to leave, 'but Earl soon come back.' With that he went into the room where he said people were sleeping.

Michael led the way into Earl's room, feeling for the light switch. Leila shut the door. The curtains looked dark green; at one time they had probably been light green, and they were torn at the bottom. Now they successfully blocked out all the daylight; they looked as though they had never really been opened. And the furniture in the room was sparse; an untrustworthy double bed, twin wardrobe, tall and wooden (though clothes were still scattered on the floor), and in the centre of the room a naked light bulb with no shade.

Leila sat down on the bed. Michael stood and looked at the crooked floor. Eventually Leila broke the silence. 'I'm going to wash and change Calvin.'

Michael nodded as she left the room.

When she came back Leila felt the bed with her hand. She peeled back the bedspread and the two blankets underneath it. The sheet looked quite clean so she laid Calvin down to sleep.

The noises of the children playing in the street were quite clear, as were the noises from the next room of the men snoring. At first Leila had thought it was only the one man, then she realized that she could hear two, maybe even three. She waited.

By the time the early afternoon sounds were replaced by the fiercer ones of lashing rain and cars struggling into the night, Leila was asleep and curled up next to her son. Michael spread himself out at the foot of the bed. He fought a long battle to stay awake and vigilant, but eventually the room tilted to the left and the naked light bulb slipped from the ceiling, and he too was asleep.

Earl was a thin man and he looked as if life had done more than its fair share of living in his small body. His speech was thick, his stance uneasy, his clothes shabby but unique. He wore a suit that was slightly too big in the arms and legs, a tie that sprouted away from his chest like a bent aerial, and a hat that looked as if it had been shrunk in the rain. He staggered noisily and pushed at Michael, who sat up and looked. Leila just turned and opened her eyes.

'Well, what happen to you all? I've been waiting since twelve o'clock down by the station.'

'We were there,' said Michael, rubbing his face.

'Well, I miss you then,' said Earl, 'and you been waiting all this time for me to come back?'

'We managed to fit in a little sleep,' said Michael.

'So I notice, man. So I notice.' He laughed, then hushed himself up. 'Don't want to wake up the lodgers.' He could see they looked puzzled. 'It's my business. I have my own room here and I watch over chaps. In the daytime I usually follow a few horses, or have a drink or something.'

'What about my mother?' Leila twisted around so that her legs fell from off the side of the bed. 'The man who let us in told me she was in a hospital.'

'Sure she in hospital. Sure, sure, but you sounding a little confused so I guess I better tell you what happen. You see, I was down there at the station waiting to see if I spy a young boy who wants a bed in a flat, and I looked at the lady and I'm thinking I do know her for true. So I edge forward a bit and I catch her eye, and she catch mine, and suddenly it dawns on the pair of us that neither one of us know who the hell the other one be. I had to laugh, man.' Earl paused for breath. He went on. 'Anyhow, I don't know why, maybe it's because she don't look too healthy, but I just ask her if she have any place as yet to stay, and she must trust me for she say ''no''. I say, well come then, I have a place. It's only when I get her on the bus that I realize I can't put her in the spare bed with the other fellers so it looks like I have to move out of my own home and stay by a next friend, so that's what happen till her health begin to really give up and the doctor find an emergency bed for her in the hospital.' Again Earl paused. ''But don't worry, I go down and see to her from time to time.'

Calvin woke up and Leila took him into her arms.

'You can go to see her first thing in the morning. It's only a short bus ride away.' Earl smiled broadly at Leila who stared back at him. She spoke into his smile.

'I want to sleep and I have to feed my child.'

'Well, I done a bit of thinking about this,' began Earl, 'and I think the best thing is for myself and your husband to sleep in here, head to foot. You and the child can sleep in the bathroom. It's alright, for you can lock the door so there don't be nobody who can get in.'

Leila followed Earl into the bathroom where he arranged the bedspread in the bath. He left the blanket on the floor for her to pull over herself once she was ready. He noticed that one item of luxury was missing.

'I going get you a pillow.' He dashed out but was back in a few seconds. 'I have it.' He placed it at the end of the bath, away from the taps.

'We don't want you getting a drip on your head in the night.' He laughed. 'I see you in the morning.'

Leila said nothing. She locked the door behind him and sat on the side of the bath. She would have to sleep in what she had on. Her other clothes were in the suitcase, but she was not going back to that room. And as she sat, her thoughts dissolved. But the nonsense of her confusion only puzzled her further; it was too soon to make or expect sense. At this stage all she knew was that her mother had lied to her or protected her, for she had not mentioned an Earl in her letters, or said anything about the place in which she lived. Maybe it was her own fault but Leila had always imagined her mother just resting up in a nice house with a special doctor coming to visit her and nurse her back to health. The shock of what she had found made her wonder what else her mother had left unsaid. It made her wonder if tomorrow would throw up some discovery more awful than this one. As she closed her eyes she simply waited, knowing she would sleep very little. On top of it all the room was cold, the enamel bath freezing, the bedspread too old and too thin to block out the chilliness. She found herself having to cradle Calvin in a position so uncomfortable that her arms were soon numb.

The next day Earl told them how to get to the hospital, but he chose not to make the journey himself. Michael, in turn, chose not to stay once he had arrived, preferring to 'go for a walk'. And after her first unsuccessful conversation (more an interview) with her mother, the nurse took Leila to another part of the hospital where she said 'the doctor' wanted to talk with her, even though Leila had expressed no desire to talk with him.

He greeted her warmly, then shut the door. He was a thin man. Leila looked closely into his face and saw the creases and folds in his middle-aged skin which reminded her of an old and beaten goat-hide.

'Please, take a seat, Mrs Preston. Your mother's asleep now and she probably won't wake up until the morning.'

He gestured her to the low seat on the other side of his desk and he swung playfully on his swivel chair.

'I assure you there's no point in your staying with her any longer.' Leila sat in silence.

'I can see from your mother's face that she's glad to see you here.' He smiled. Leila watched him and waited.

'Look, I don't wish to make it any more painful than it already is, but the simple fact of the matter is that your mother is very seriously ill.' The doctor's voice became more resonant and distant.

'It all depends upon her strength of mind, but I think I can honestly say that your coming here will do her the world of good.'

Leila looked at him, this awkward man, knowing he did not care, though she could not as yet prove it.

'All I can say, Mrs Preston, is that the medical profession is not an . . .'

Leila stood up and, holding Calvin with one arm, she turned away from the desk.

'Please, Mrs Preston.' The doctor stood. But Leila had already left the room.

He reminded her of the men for whom she had worked at Government Headquarters, the white men, who spoke to her with a smile on their face as if afraid that to release it might be interpreted as sexual aggression, or colonial bullying, or both. And so the sugary smile became a part of their uniform, and whenever Leila saw it she knew that behind it a man was frightened, not of her but of himself, and she hated cowards.

Michael was waiting for her by the entrance to the hospital. He had finished his walk and he stood leaning against the white wall and listening to the low droning of an invisible piece of hospital equipment.

Once back at the flat Earl went to make them both a cup of tea. Leila said nothing and again Michael came over to her.

'You want to come and look for a place to live, for I thought we could do that this afternoon?'

She shook her head. Earl came in with the tea. He had overheard. 'Don't worry,' he assured Michael. 'It's only two o'clock, plenty of time.'

Leila looked up at them both and then down at her inadequate sandals and the threadbare carpet. For most of the afternoon they sat in silence. Then Earl made a long overdue excuse about 'business' and reluctantly left his own flat.

For a few minutes Michael stared into space, watching the light fail. Then Leila got up and changed and fed their son. The noises from the street eventually faded away, as did the daylight. Then the lodgers from the day shift came home to sleep, and the night workers left their unmade beds. Then it was quiet again and there was no longer anything for them to think about except this day slipping away into tomorrow and yet another new beginning.

Leila peeled the bedspread back from off the bed and Michael, standing near the window, turned to look at her. She began to undress.

'She's going to die. The doctor at the hospital wouldn't tell me, but I know.'

Michael began to take off his clothes and prepare for bed. He moved the sleeping Calvin to one side and, as he folded Leila into his arms, she smelt the stale smoke which had become trapped in the tight curls of his hair.

It was almost one o'clock in the morning when a drunken Earl came back. He kicked off his shoes but only stopped singing when he realized that Leila was in the bed too. He crept out of the room. The door to the bathroom was locked.

Earl stood and shivered in the cluttered hallway until its occupant had finished.

The next morning Leila stood by the window and bounced Calvin up and down in her arms. Below her a car shot swiftly through the puddles. It had rained all night. Earl went on, 'I got a hangover like someone trying to bury their damn way out of my skull. English beer is something else, boy, something else.'

Michael laughed, and Earl cleared his throat. He could see Leila looking at him. He spoke nervously to her.

'First of all I was thinking that we can take a stroll around by the park area where there is quite a lot of rooms to let. Then you and the child can go down by the hospital and visit your mother, while your husband and myself can go and look for a job for him. Alright so far?'

Leila said nothing.

'Anyhow, after you finish at the hospital we can all meet up back here and if we don't find nowhere to live as yet then we should just walk some more until we can see what we can find.'

Leila still remained silent.

They walked slowly, Leila noticing that it was slightly colder than the previous day, and they followed the half-deserted morning streets which were decorated with drifting strands of fog. Leila had listened to Earl referring to this as the park area but there did not seem to be any sign of either tree or vegetation in the run-down back streets through which they passed. Large white women stood on well-washed doorsteps, their arms folded over dirty aprons, their cigarettes drooping lazily out of the corners of their slanted mouths, and they watched them, keeping a wary eye on their own children, or somebody else's children, while talking loudly to each other. The cold did not seem to bother these women, and the presence of coloured people signalled only a momentary lull in their staccato conversations.

Michael thrust his hands deep into his trouser pockets.

'You want me carry the child?'

Calvin was awake and restless, but Leila could manage.

'No.'

'I think we should maybe start trying from here onwards,' said Earl, his thin body almost invisible underneath his bulk of clothes. 'There's usually a few signs round these parts.'

Michael agreed.

Leila followed as they turned abruptly into a long straight road with houses along one side only. On the other side of the road was a high steel-wire fence and behind it were tractors and bulldozers and building equipment. The ground was churned up and the men seemed like ants doing their little jobs in busy isolation. This must be the park, thought Leila. They walked along this empty road looking up to their left for signs, but the first three they saw gave Leila an idea as to what to expect. 'No coloureds', 'No vacancies', 'No children'. Nobody said anything and they walked on. Then, twenty yards down the road, they saw a hastily scribbled sign on a piece of cardboard that had been thrust into the downstairs window of a house. 'We have vacancies', it announced confidently.

'This looks like a place for us,' said Earl.

They climbed the half dozen steps and Earl knocked loudly at the door. A white woman in her fifties, small, well-dressed and with her hair carefully brushed back, stood before the three adults and the child. She spoke first, giving them no time to state their business.

'I'm sorry, but it's only a small room and I can't take all of you.' She moved as if she was going to shut the door but Earl leaned forward.

'But it's just for my friends here. A married couple.'

For a moment the woman looked hesitant, her eyes meeting Leila's. Then she broke contact.

'Look, I'm sorry, but it's only a small room and I really don't want any couples or babies.'

Earl continued to argue, but Leila turned and walked back down the steps. The woman's eyes followed her, and Leila now stood with her back to them, looking out across the road. As Earl began a new sentence the door slammed.

Five houses further down the road there was another sign. It too looked hastily written. 'Rooms to let'. Earl rang the bell and a younger woman of about thirty answered the door. She kept her composure, raising just the one eyebrow.

'Hello. I expect you've come about the rooms, but I'm afraid I can't make any decision until I've talked with my husband, and he's not here at the moment, and anyway the rooms are occupied at the present time. It was the future that we were thinking of, so if it's now that you're thinking of moving in somewhere then I'm awfully sorry but we just can't help you at this particular moment.' She smiled, or rather beamed, as she closed the door.

They walked a little slower now, but the rest of the signs were explicit. 'No vacancies for coloureds'. 'No blacks'. 'No coloureds'. Leila felt grateful for their honesty. Earl was philosophical about the whole thing.

'Well, some people just don't like us and I guess we have to deal with it.'

At the end of the road Earl stopped.

'Look, you see this bus coming.' He spoke quickly to Leila. 'You can get a threepenny from here to the hospital. Just keep looking out of the window and you going see it on your left after you pass over a big roundabout. Then this afternoon it's the same bus you get back to here. We should be back before you so don't worry about knocking anyone up.'

Leila listened carefully. Then she climbed aboard the bus. It did not take long to get to the hospital.

Leila sat for over an hour with her mother, who slept with her mouth open, clearly still finding it difficult to breathe. She held Calvin close, hoping he would not cry out and wake up his grandmother. Then the nurse came in with a cup of tea.

156

After Leila had drunk it the nurse whispered she would like to speak with her in the corridor. Leila left her mother, knowing that she would not wake up for at least a few hours more.

'The doctor is very concerned over the way in which you left yesterday.'

Leila looked at the woman, not caring what she or the doctor thought.

'Do you have an address or a telephone number where we might contact you quickly if we need to?'

Leila shook her head.

'Are you looking for somewhere to live?'

'Yes.'

'I see,' said the nurse. 'It's difficult these days.' She paused. 'Look, I rent a small flat from an estate agency in Marble Arch. I know they have properties, so I could let you have their address if you like, and I'd be happy to let you use me as a referee.'

'Thank you.'

The nurse disappeared. She came back and gave Leila a card.

'It's really easy to find. You just get on a number 6 bus and ask the conductor to put you off at the stop before Marble Arch. Then it's right there on the left. Just show them this card with my name and I'm sure it'll be alright.'

Leila listened and wondered. Then, when the nurse had finished, she went back in and sat with her sleeping mother.

She asked to be put off the bus at the stop before Marble Arch, and the conductor came to her personally and told her when it was time, and how to get to the estate agent's, and she thanked him. Leila pushed open the door and stepped forward on to the carpet, which was so soft and deep she felt as though she was going to fall with every step she took. The woman behind the desk looked up and knocked the ash from her cigarette into an ugly thick ashtray.

'Yes, madam, can I help you?'

Calvin fought with her and Leila nearly lost hold of him.

'Please, take a seat as we don't want you to drop the baby now, do we?'

Leila sat down. She handed the woman the card. She looked at it and gave it back to Leila. It did not seem to be important.

'And what is it that we can do for you, Mrs . . .'

'Mrs Preston.'

The receptionist stubbed out her cigarette and turned her attention to picking her teeth. Leila noticed that the woman's teeth were crooked and too big for her mouth.

'I'm looking for somewhere to live.'

'For just yourself and the baby?'

'No, for my husband too.'

'I see. Well, we have somewhere that I think you might find suitable. It's a small house, a terraced property, near to a bus stop and shops, and close to the schools so you can be assured that it has all the conveniences. The rent is very reasonable at £3 a week. Interested?'

Leila nodded.

'Fine.' The receptionist picked up the telephone. 'I won't be a moment.' She dialled a number and waited a few seconds before speaking. As she waited she curled a watery smile in Calvin's direction. Then she had her short conversation and put down the telephone.

'It's awfully cold for this time of the year,' said the woman, flicking disinterestedly through a diary on her desk.

'Yes,' said Leila, and together they waited.

'Mrs Preston.' He stretched out his friendly hand to greet her.

'My name is Jansen and I understand that you're interested in our Florence Road property.'

'Yes.'

'Good. Well, the property is available immediately which, as I'm sure you understand, is very unusual. You need only pay us £12, which is a month's rent in advance. If that's alright with you we can draw up the lease this afternoon, you can come in with the money in the morning, then we can give you the keys and you can be well and truly installed by this time tomorrow. Do we have an agreement?'

'Yes, thank you.'

Mr Jansen beamed cheerily. 'Right, then, we'll see you tomorrow morning.'

Leila hesitated. 'About nine o'clock?' she asked.

'Just fine.' Mr Jansen held the door open for her.

Leila stood in the street, suddenly realizing that she would have to go all the way back to the hospital to catch the bus back to Earl's. This was complicated, but at least she had ensured that this would be their last night with Earl whom, almost without realizing it, she had come to loathe.

'When you move in?' asked Earl.

Michael cleared his throat. 'Tomorrow. We pick up the key in the morning according to Leila.'

Earl stood up. 'I guess you all better go out tonight and celebrate, for even though you still don't have a job you really arrive in England now. I can babysit for you.'

Leila wiped some food from Calvin's mouth. Michael stood up and went across to Earl and extended his hand, but Earl turned away from him like a spurned wife.

'I just want to say thank you for looking after us.'

Earl laughed. 'Now wait, you mean to say you think that is it? It's over now and you can deal with this country on your own.?'

Michael looked puzzled. Then Earl laughed again and slapped him on the shoulder. 'You two go out and have a good time. You both deserve it.'

At the time when things were normally stopping back home they were just beginning in England. The night was wet after rain, and the glare from the streetlights dazzled. They were going to the cinema. Sheltering in the doorways they walked past, Leila saw men huddled together, collars erect, bodies

159

shivering, hands striking matches to burnt-out cigarettes, and in the brief flicker she could see the stubble that lay thick on their faces like a salty mask.

The shaft of light crashed through the rising smoke. The colour and noises left Michael spellbound for the full three hours of the film. In the darkness Leila cried, for her mother. And then it was over.

As they got off the bus she looked up in momentary alarm. The sky hung so low it covered the street like a dark coffin lid. The cars that passed by were just blurry colours, and the people rushed homeward, images of isolation, fighting umbrellas and winds that buffeted their bodies. Leila wanted to sleep, wanted the day to end painlessly so she could begin again tomorrow. They walked home in silence.

It was sunny outside as Leila took Calvin, and Michael took the suitcase, and they made their way to the estate agent's to sign the lease and pick up the keys. Then they went to the tube station where they would begin the real journey. As Leila signed the lease she had made sure that her writing was more than just a name, it was a signature.

The underground frightened Leila, and Calvin cried. But, beside the ever-present fear that they might have got on the wrong tube, there was also the fear that the train was going so fast that it would not be able to stop. Each time it braked they seemed to be already halfway out of the station, and they held on to the straps and swung back and forth into each other until they reached the end of the line.

On stepping back into the daylight, the houses offered precious little comfort to Leila's eyes. Like Earl's neighbourhood they disappointed in their filth. Unlike Earl's neighbourhood they were small, clearly cramped and uncomfortable, even on the outside. Again they were all joined up, and although Number One, Florence Road was not hard to find it was hard to believe.

It stood at the corner of a main street which ran downhill and away under a railway bridge, and a side-terraced street that ran dead into a brick wall. Leila stood at this junction and looked up at their home. Two of the upstairs window panes were broken in, and the door looked like it had been put together from the remains of a dozen forgotten doors. Like the street down by the park where Earl had taken them yesterday morning, the women stood, arms crossed, out on their doorsteps, and they watched the newcomers' every move. Luckily, thought Leila, children played safely in this street, for the traffic was easy to control as it came only from one direction.

Michael pushed the key into the door, opened it and groped the wall. The light switch did not work. The house was dark and smelled of neglect, and there were no curtains to open to let the light in, and there were no doors to prop open to let the air circulate. In the living room there was an old settee, an empty fireplace and a table so scratched and battered that it looked as if someone had made a bad job of shaving it. Michael put down the suitcase and went to open a window. He strained and pushed till the veins stood out on the side of his head, but it would not open. Leila stood in the centre of the room and rocked Calvin in her arms. Michael gave up and turned and walked past her.

'I'm going to take a look upstairs.'

Leila heard him but she looked away through the dirty and stubborn window.

Upstairs there was a solitary bedroom. A soiled double mattress lay prostrate in the middle of an otherwise naked floor. The two broken panes of glass stared at Michael and he slammed the door behind him in anger. The small bathroom consisted of a toilet bowl and a wash basin. That was all. There was no bath, and the door to this room hung from its hinges. What looked like a door to another room turned out to be a cupboard, and it was in here that the water heater was. Michael made his way down the wooden steps and into the front room. Leila had not moved. He strode to the far side of the front room.

The kitchen was small and filthy. The cooker looked as though it had never been cleaned in its life. It was complemented by a set of ill-matching and ill-fitting cupboards, some full of dirt and empty packets, some bare. He left the kitchen.

'They tell you what this place was like before you handed over the money?'

Leila looked across the room at him. 'They told me it was a terraced property near to the shops and all the conveniences.' Leila turned Calvin over in her arms.

'Well, when you done take a good look at your terraced property I think you better think again about whether decent people can be expected to live in a place like this.' Michael pushed his fingertips into one of the damp patches on the wall. 'We don't travel halfway around the world to live in a place like this.'

'It was all they had.'

'Well, it won't do.'

Again Leila turned and looked out of the window.

'I'm going out to seek some work but I don't expect to find the place like this when I come back.' Michael moved past her.

'I have to go to the hospital,' said Leila.

He slammed the front door and Leila remained still, feeling suddenly cold, like last night when she had felt cold in the bathroom, unable to decide if the greater mistake was coming to England or agreeing to spend a third night by Earl.

Leila waited a few minutes, then sat down and wondered about her mother, whom she knew she would not see today; but this was hardly solace for her mind and she felt angry, not so much at Michael's disappearance but at the fact of his blaming her for the state of the house. After all, neither he nor Earl had found a place, and despite the state of the property it had a roof and four walls, and for a while, at least, was theirs.

As the sun began to catch the filth on the windows Leila blinked vigorously, then rubbed her eyes. Though she saw again the filth on the glass the day was brighter now, but also dirtier, and she felt sleep creeping back into her body.

It was on the train coming up to London that Leila had realized all her old worries about Michael were now much more intense. Two weeks of non-communication on the ship had only served to deepen her distress. So much between them still remained unspoken. Back home, before they were married, but after she had agreed to marry him, they had sat together for almost a whole day just looking down the street at nothing in particular, but without speaking. As hour after hour slipped by, Leila grew more anxious until she finally recognized this state of anxiety as one she lived in perpetually, his silence baffling and hurtful, his moods unpredictable, his distrust obvious and murdering any chance of a durable base to their relationship.

Then Michael had stood up and walked away a few paces, his hands in his pockets, his feet playing loosely with the dust. The sun was setting.

'I think I better go back down to Sandy Bay now,' he said. Leila squinted and tried to shield the sun from her eyes. She stared into the back of his head.

'Alright,' she said. 'Are you going to come up tomorrow after I've been to church?'

'Maybe,' said Michael. 'It depends on how Bradeth's feeling. Things are a bit slow at the moment, so maybe he don't want no work doing.'

From inside the house they both heard Leila's mother cough and then it was quiet again.

'I better go now.'

He did not turn around to look at Leila, or come and kiss her. It was as if there was something on his mind of which she was no part; he simply shut her out, left her on the ground like an extra nut, his mind having spent the day assembling the other pieces.

Slowly, as Michael rode down the road and into the bend and out of sight, Leila stood. She went through to her mother's bedroom to see how she might help, but her mother was asleep and had merely coughed without knowing it.

And now the two-week passage seemed to have reintroduced her to the unhappiness she felt on that day, and on many others like it. It made a nonsense of their reunion, for her marriage was again to be tolerated, not shared. It seemed to her that no matter what she said or did Michael had decided to give her nothing in return, except for his anger or his all too familiar silence. But Leila preferred this to conflict, fearful that her mother might think her a failure if they were to separate yet again.

On her first night in their new home Leila lay in bed alone. She could hear Michael outside the front door feeling for the key in his pocket. But he had forgotten his key and she had left the door open. In his absence Leila had worked unceasingly and now every muscle in her body ached.

The cupboard doors were either put back on their old hinges or taken off completely. It looked neater that way. The windows were washed and the floor swept clean. She found an old bedspread which she draped over the settee in the front room. It was now alright to sit on it. Leila gave the crooked shaven table a tablecloth for a companion, and around it there stood three proud but shaky wooden chairs. Most important of all, she had started a fire burning in the grate and put a bundle of wooden staves in a metal pail so the house would be warm.

In the bedroom the mattress was now covered with a bedspread, with sheets, with blankets. The two pillows were in pillowcases. The broken panes were neatly covered by cardboard. The panes that were intact were clean. The room had curtains and a lampshade, it had a bedside table and a cot for Calvin (which he was sleeping in at the moment). Leila watched over him and made sure he slept peacefully.

'Leila!' Michael shouted, but though Leila heard him she did not answer. For the past hour she had lain in bed staring at the ceiling whose cracks looked aged, like the veins on a dead leaf.

'Aggh?'

She heard him fall over and she sat bolt upright. She looked to make sure he had not woken up Calvin. The moonlight crept into the room and she lowered herself back into bed and waited. Calvin was still asleep.

Michael held one hand against his temple and swore. He had hurt his head as he fell through the door. He sat on the settee and looked at the glowing embers in the fireplace until his head stopped spinning. Then he launched himself upright and began to stumble upstairs. He turned the lights on in the bedroom.

'It's the right house I'm in or what?'

Leila did not answer. She pretended to be asleep, and Michael sucked his teeth, then turned out the light before taking off his clothes and sliding into bed beside her.

'Leila', he whispered, breathing beer into her ear. But she was sleeping. So he propped himself up and breathed it into her face.

'Leila?' Michael forced his hand down between her legs and prised them open. Then he hauled himself on top of her, unable to take any of the weight himself. As Leila moved, scared she would be crushed, Michael again reached down his hand. But it was no good. He leaned over and vomited beside her head, catching the edge of the pillow and running back some of the vomit into her hair. Then, having emptied his stomach for a third time, he lay unconscious and draped across her like a dead whale. Leila heard him beginning to snore but she dare not, in fact could not move. She looked at the side of his head and waited until morning came. But, when morning did come, Leila was finally asleep and Michael left the house without waking her up.

Michael climbed past the flat caps, through the mud-caked boots, and went to sit on the top deck of the bus. Across the aisle from him were two men, both of whom were as fat as armchairs and both of whom had veins and moles sketched on their faces in random patterns of ugliness. Michael thought they must be brothers. He arched forward and looked out of the window. Then a sudden escaping cloud lit up the cold day. He thought this might be a good sign for the interview.

The girl was painting her nails. She sat, one leg tucked underneath the other, behind a desk with a bulky typewriter on it. Her face looked like a mask, her features simple and hard.

'You saw the job in the paper?'

Michael nodded. She tossed her head in frustration.

'Well, go on. Go on in or are you waiting for something?'

Michael sat on the near side of the man's cluttered desk and felt the silent mockery. Occasionally Mr Jeffries (his name was on a plaque) took a drink from the cracked mug of tea that stood by his right hand, but it was a few moments before he addressed Michael directly.

'Have you ever been to prison or to a courtroom in front of a judge?'

Michael shook his head.

'How many wives, one or two?'

'One.'

Mr Jeffries smashed his cigarette dead and smiled gently. Michael followed the slight curl of the man's lips.

'You're ready to start straight away, are you?'

Michael nodded and Mr Jeffries stood up. For a large man he moved easily, as if his shoes were made of velvet, the carpet of some cloud-like material. Without turning around Michael had no idea of how close to him the man was.

'Follow me.'

166

Michael stood.

As they crossed the courtyard Mr Jeffries shouted to an Englishman in overalls, 'You can put up the 'COLOURED QUOTA FULL' sign now.'

The man turned his thumb skyward.

As they neared the large brick building Mr Jeffries began to speak again.

'Now then, do you know what a paper clip is?'

Michael nodded.

'Well, all you have to do is to scoop up as many of them as you can hold in your left hand, and holding a small box in the other hand, put them in. I hope you've got that.'

Again Michael nodded.

'Now, I don't expect . . .'

Suddenly the man's words were drowned by the noise of thundering machines. Mr Jeffries looked around, then gestured with both arms to the only other coloured man in the building. Michael's ears began to hurt.

The tea break was to last fifteen minutes and Edwin went to get them both a cup of tea. He was a short man with a bald patch shining in the middle of his head which made him look like a powerful black monk. His nylon shirt was buttoned from the collar down to his chest, then for some reason it buttoned no further and just flared out into a tent-like finish. His pants were held up by a belt which seemed to bear no relation to the loops that were there for it to be threaded through. He looked casual, but affable, and he returned with two hot dirty-looking cups and sat.

'You know you do favour a chap I used to know, but them is the sort of people who come from nothing back home to be even bigger nothings over here, so I glad you're not family to them.' Michael smiled nervously.

'So how long you been over here now?' asked Edwin, kicking off some dirt from his workboots.

'Close to a week now.'

'Well, all you need to remember is they treat us worse than their dogs. The women expect you to do tricks with your biceps and sing calypso, or to drop down on one knee and pretend you're Paul Robeson or somebody.'

Edwin took a long loud sip on his tea.

'English people do wear overcoats in the summer and short jackets in the winter and mark my words good, don't put no money in no chocolate machines on the tube platforms for it's just a way of robbing off a coloured man's money.'

Edwin paused and thought. Then he looked up at Michael and spoke quietly.

'Though of course you not going make any money here. And before you been in this job a week you going start dreaming of home. And I don't mean dream, dream, I mean nightmare, dream. And then, unless you watch your step, before you know it you soon be going out in the evening and meeting the kind of coloured man who like to tell everyone he's Brazilian, that he's Pelé or somebody.'

'Who's Pelé?'

'Young boy, sixteen or something, just win the World Cup for Brazil in Sweden or some place.'

Edwin paused a moment, then grinned.

'I hear Swedish women nice, boy.' Again he paused. 'But I don't want no son of mine kicking no damn English football. He going be a cricketer, like his father.' Edwin was interrupted by the screaming of a hooter. He stood and encouraged Michael to finish his tea.

'By the way, what you think of Jeffries?'

'I don't know,' said Michael, draining the cup.

Edwin took the cup and laughed.

'Well, you better know. He's a cunt and he's going to call you names, man, and you going to behave like a kettle for without knowing it you going to boil. It's how the white man in this country kills off the coloured man. He makes you heat up and blow yourself away.'

That evening Michael joined Edwin and his two friends at the newly opened Caribbean Club. Edwin had said that he preferred it to the pub, and as they eased their way down the concave steps Michael heard music.

Edwin's friends sat at the far side of the dingy, deserted club. For an hour they all talked loudly. Then Edwin pushed the table away from him and shifted his glass, as if making room for plans. But there were no plans, just more idle talk.

Eventually Michael left the club and stepped out into the black night. The driving rain lashed down, only visible when it speared past the lamp-posts or broke the surface of the slack water puddles. He lowered his head, turned up his collar and began running.

Back at Florence Road he fumbled noisily at the lock, unable to direct the key into the door. He sat on the doorstep, his head pounding, before trying again. His already strengthening hangover was not Edwin's fault, but by tomorrow morning he would have learned how to blame Edwin. The key went in the door.

Already England was more than Michael had dared hope for. On the ship his mind had ached trying to arrange the words of his grandmother, the memory of his grandfather, and the warnings of Footsie Walters' brother Alphonse into a meaningful pattern. He seldom thought of Bradeth, for he doubted if he would see him again before the grey years. As he gave him the bike Michael had sensed that Bradeth knew this too. In addition, Bradeth had neither the wisdom of age nor the luxury of experience to help now, so Michael put him to the back of his mind. It was the immediate future he found himself having to deal with, not the past. But as the days slipped by, and the ship edged its way towards England, Michael came to admit that his future might not include Leila, in the same way that his present did not include Beverley. If England was the place that Alphonse Walters had led him to believe it was, then how much energy could he afford to waste continually patching up this newly repaired but still leaky marriage? The more he thought about it, the more he realized the nurturing and pretence would have to stop. On the threshold of a new life, he could not afford to fail in fulfilling the wishes of his grandparents.

And now, as he began to drag himself up the stairs, he could hardly wait for the next day to begin. Michael spun the ring his grandmother had given him around on his finger, and again he thought of his grandfather. There was no chance of his leaving this country with nothing, that was certain. How much he left with seemed to depend totally upon how much he wanted, and how hard he was prepared to try. This being the case Michael would sleep soundly and defend his mind against thoughts of Beverley or Leila or the children.

*

It was some weeks later that Leila put the cup of tea in front of her neighbour, ashamed that she had nothing better in which to give it to her. She had called around to see if she could offer Leila any help but, as the minutes ticked by and the woman relaxed, it became clear that she really wanted to talk. Leila did not resent this.

'Well, what did you think it would be like?' asked Mary, as she put more wood on to the fire.

'I don't really know. I thought it would be much warmer than this.'

'Ah, well, there you are. This is the summer and you just wait till you get to January and February. It was awful last year. I used to say to Harry – Harry's my husband – I used to come home and say to him how I'd seen some of you, coloureds that is, shivering by the bus stops and I just wanted to go across and hug you and say, "don't worry, love, you'll get used to it."' She laughed. 'I never did, though.'

'What does Harry do?'

'Oh, he does alright for himself these days. He works in a factory, foreman though, but he used to have a stall on the market when I first met him. And then there was the war when he was overseas, France most of the time. You do know about the war, don't you?'

Leila smiled. For a moment Mary did not know whether to be embarrassed or annoyed. In the end she was neither as she just stared at the laughing girl.

'I was only small when the war was happening, so I don't remember much, but they told us about it at school.'

'What I meant, though, was that you didn't have any actual fighting where you were, did you, or did you?'

'No, but I think we used to see the planes going overhead sometimes, German ones as well. My mother used to tell me they were just big flies in case I was frightened. But other people in my village used to dance around singing, "Jerry, Jerry, Jerry." The bigger ones, that is.'

The fire began to rise and its glow caught Mary's face and picked out the lines of her age.

'You used to live in a village?'

Leila nodded, unsure as to whether she had ended their friendship by her confession.

'What was its name?'

'St Patrick's, after the Irish saint. I think there must have been some Irish people there at some point.'

'You mean some Irish people used to live in your village?'

Leila looked at Mary and wondered to herself how she was possibly going to explain this. At school her teachers had already done their best to confuse what little history of the island there was, and she had never really worked out for herself the relationship between the English, the Irish, the French, the Portuguese, the Africans and so on. The teachers had talked about each group as if it had made the most important contribution to the history of the island. If Leila said to Mary that Irish people had been there, then she knew she would be giving the wrong picture, even though they had, but she could not really tell the truth. It was too complicated, even for her.

'Some Irish people used to live there, a long time ago, but I don't think any do now.'

'Were they eaten? I don't mean now, I mean a long time ago,' asked Mary. 'They might have done something wrong.'

'I don't think anybody ever ate anybody whatever they did,' said Leila, 'but they used to kill each other.'

'Just like the war over here. Though God only knows what some of them got up to in the desert. I wouldn't be at all surprised if that lot ate each other.'

Mary came and sat down by Leila. She stretched her legs, rubbed her thighs and sighed. Then she began to chuckle.

'You know, this reminds me so much of when I moved in with Harry into our house. We thought we'd won the bloody pools.'

'The what?'

'The pools. The football pools. Don't worry about it. It's just a funny way we folk have of throwing our money down the drain every week and hoping some of it will come flooding out when we turn the taps on.'

Again she laughed to herself.

'Do you have any children?' asked Leila.

'Hah! Do I have any kids? Two of the beggars, though, they're at an age now when I shouldn't have to worry too much about them. The oldest one, Kevin, he's twenty, and Val's sixteen. They've both got jobs, and a home, and boyfriends and girlfriends, but from the way they go on you'd think we were back in the thirties all of a sudden. The world at their bloody feet and all they do is moan, or in the case of our Kevin, moan and dress up like a bloody clown in his teddy boy gear. You want to be thankful you've only got one and he's not big enough to answer you back as yet. If I were you I'd start to train him up now. Buy a big stick and everytime he opens his mouth clock him one on the head. That'll save you so much trouble you'll thank me in ten years' time.'

They both laughed, and Leila looked across at Mary who closed her eyes, though her shoulders still rippled. She was friendly and helpful, but she puzzled Leila, for she could not work out why she would want to be so towards a total stranger. But then Leila thought of home, and what would happen if Mary had moved into St Patrick's with her family, or into Sandy Bay, or any place on the island, and suddenly it did not seem so strange.

That afternoon they went shopping and Mary's shopping bag looked as if it was going to burst at the seams. Leila could carry no more, both arms stretched and still stretching, making her feel sure that if she did not put down her bags her knuckles would soon be scraping the sidewalk.

'Look, love, I can't go any further.' Mary slumped on to the bonnet of a parked car. She rested her feet up on the rear bumper of the one in front of it.

'It's alright for you but I'm an old woman, Leila. There's hardly any life left in these old pegs now.'

'You're not old,' said Leila, as she rested down her bags on the bonnet with Mary's. 'You're just tired. We must have walked miles.'

'We've walked a mile and been pushed three, I reckon. Let's get out of this madness and have a cup of tea.'

Leila watched as Mary slipped off a shoe, squeezed her toes, then slipped her shoe back on. She did the same with her other foot, then stood up and picked up her bag.

'Well, come on then, I'm the tired one, remember.'

Leila grabbed at her bags and tagged on to Mary like a daughter to a mother.

The café was almost empty. They sat heavily. At first the young girl behind the tureens and yards of silver piping seemed oblivious to their presence. The girl wiped her nose on the sleeve of her once white coat. Then she emptied some rusty looking tea out of a huge tin pot and into one of the sinks before making theirs.

'No doubt by the time I get back Kevin'll be complaining about his food and Harry will be sat there looking at me as if it's nothing to do with him.'

Mary took a sip of her tea and went on, 'My mother was right. "It'll take the war for the buggers to realize how important we are," she used to say, "but as soon as Hitler hangs his clogs up we'll be back skivvying and scurrying like there's nothing in our heads."'

They sat together, Leila drinking her second cup of tea and trying to imagine what Mary and Harry talked about when they were alone; Mary staring out through the steamed-up window. Then Leila touched Mary on the arm and threw her back into the world.

'Have I been asleep?'

'No, just daydreaming,' said Leila.

Mary stood and picked up her heavy bag. She opened the door and the roar of the rush hour traffic startled them.

At home Leila dropped her two bags on the kitchen floor and took Calvin to sleep upstairs. Then she made herself a coffee and again she waited for Michael, whose remoteness continued to grow with every day. These days he just seemed to use the house as a place in which to change his shoes and clothes. What it was he was thinking she had no idea, and whether or not she could be of any assistance to him seemed, at this stage, an irrelevancy. In England, and without Beverley, he still did not want her. But until he spoke with her she would let him remain as a passenger on the same train, in the same carriage. She knew she would have to wait to find out his destination, unless of course something forced her to get off the train before him.

174

It was some weeks later that Leila noticed people were beginning to retreat into themselves and wear long coats. The leaves were falling from the trees.

At the hospital the nurse held Leila by the shoulder and whispered she had better go now as her mother needed some sleep. She also told her that there was someone here to see her. Leila walked slowly out of the ward, glancing back all the time. She always got the impression her mother was fooling with her, that she was not really tired and she just felt what had to be said had been said. But, as Leila neared the door, she looked again at her mother. There was no sign of mischief in her face, and no sign that the relationship Leila had dreamed of for so long would ever materialize.

Earl stood in the corridor, his face heavy. Untidy and stooping, this was not the Earl who had so confidently introduced them to London. Leila could see he had been drinking. She could smell it.

'I'll leave the pair of you to it,' said the nurse. She spoke to Leila. 'I'll be around the corner if you need me.'

Earl waited until the nurse left.

'How is your mother?'

'Tired,' said Leila. 'Apart from that she's fine.'

'Good.'

Leila waited for him to carry on, but he just looked at her. As she steadied herself to leave, Earl began to speak.

'You hear of the department of public health, like sanitary inspectors back home?' Leila nodded. 'They say I must have only two lodgers.' He paused. 'I lost my business to the people.' Earl shifted his weight from one foot to the other. 'Maybe you would like a cup of coffee at the flat?'

'I have to pick up Calvin from the lady next door.'

Earl understood.

'Well, maybe I see you later then?'

Leila turned and left.

Leila went to bed alone. She thought of Earl and felt uneasy. She switched off the light and settled down. Of late Calvin seemed to be sleeping right through the night, but Leila lay in darkness knowing that at some point Michael would come in, wake her and perhaps try and quarrel. These days she waited, for she hated being woken up and then not being able to get back to sleep. But, against her will, she fell asleep and for the first time she woke up in the morning still alone.

Leila dashed downstairs and found Michael on the settee. Even though he was still sleeping he looked angry and moody. She wandered into the kitchen where she made Calvin's food and a pot of tea. Michael heard her. He rubbed his face and sat upright. He had a hangover.

'Tea?' shouted Leila. Her voice betrayed no anxiety. Michael nodded gently, even though she could not see him. Leila brought the tea and he drank it but said nothing. She was upstairs bathing Calvin in the sink when Michael left for work. Leila heard the door slam.

That afternoon Leila looked at her mother across a crowded ward. She could see she was in a deep sleep. When she woke up her mother's conversation was odd. She spoke of beatings, and asked if Michael had ever beaten her. Again Leila wondered if her mother was going to die in England, but the thought was banished as soon as it appeared.

That night it was Leila's turn to sleep on the settee. She did not mean to but she just fell asleep there; and when she woke in the morning, and heard the children playing in the street, she knew a new day was beginning.

She took Michael a coffee and he began to drink it as if nothing was the matter, as if he had not noticed that his wife had not slept beside him. He lit a cigarette and blew a premature cloud of smoke. Leila took Calvin out of his cot and cradled him in her arms. Then she crossed the room and looked out of the window.

'You're late for work.'

Michael laughed. She heard him resting down the cup on the floor by the bed.

'I've decided to give up work now. Edwin and myself are thinking of going into business together.'

'Business?' asked Leila, turning to face him. 'What kind of business?'

'We don't know as yet. We still have to discuss it, this morning maybe.'

'How are we going to live until this business materializes?' Leila spoke quickly, as if already arguing.

But Michael, having finished his coffee, slid his naked frame out of bed. Leila looked at him as he first put out his cigarette, then touched his toes as if anxious to demonstrate his flexibility.

'You see, you don't got no ambition, girl. You come to this country just to sit in this house and play with the child? Well? You come here to push pram around London with the old woman next door?' Leila turned away from him.

'You don't want to look, then don't frigging look. What you can see is good enough for some people even if you don't think so.'

Leila felt as though someone had struck her. Michael went on, 'Why you can't back me up like any wife should do? Why you can't say, Michael, I think it's a good idea, or Michael, I'm proud of you showing some ambition and spark even though I know it's a risk, or something like that? Other fellers have wives who help them, why I must be different? Why?'

'Because,' said Leila, 'You have a wife who cares more about her child than pubs and drinking.'

'So you don't think I'm interested in Calvin or what?' Michael shouted. 'You don't think that what I'm planning is for the benefit of my son or what!'

'Is it, Michael? Is it? And if it is, why can't you talk to his mother about it?'

'Because his mother is a selfish, superior arse who think she do me a favour by marrying to me.' Michael kicked over the coffee cup. He stalked towards her.

'You know nothing about this country,' he said, pushing her back up against the wall, 'and it's maybe about time you started to ask instead of complain, to support instead of looking down your long nose at me, understand!'

Leila could feel his finger in her chest, and Calvin twisting and turning in her arms, but she dared not look Michael in the face. Then, after a long pause, longer than she thought she dared wait, she nodded, first once, then twice, then three times, just wanting him to leave her alone. Eventually he turned and walked naked from the bedroom and into the bathroom.

She waited a moment, then moved from the window. Then she bent down and picked up Michael's cup from the floor. She went downstairs to the kitchen and lit the cooker. Mary's daughter, Val, was off work this week with a cold. She would ask her to look after Calvin while she went to the hospital. Michael would no doubt go out to see to his new 'business', and she knew she could not rely upon his help. Then Leila looked up and water began to drip from the ceiling into a well-placed bowl on the kitchen floor. Michael had flushed the lavatory. A few minutes later she heard him tumble down the stairs, and then the door crash shut as he left the house.

Leila prepared herself for the journey that only seemed to depress her. After four months it had not become any easier. This time, she thought, she would try and ease her depression on the bus by calculating how many times she had visited the hospital.

WINTER

Her mother's funeral was a sad affair. Leila wore the large silver earrings she had last worn at her wedding, not knowing or caring whether it was a good thing or a bad thing to do. In the end it would seem to have been a bad thing. They stood underneath a huge oak tree, whose arms were spread out like a great umbrella trying to hold off the cold drizzle, and they stood, each holding a smaller, mushroom-like version of the tree in their hands. The nurse and the doctor shared one between them, and Earl stood apart and got wet. Harry, Mary and Val, heads bowed, looked cold and uneasy, and Harry kept glancing at his wife and daughter, but they were oblivious to his discomfort.

Michael and Leila each sheltered under their own umbrella, neither of them showing any emotion. Beneath Leila's feet the grass felt like mud and the slightest movement of foot reduced it to such. The priest opened the pages of his Bible and covered them with a plastic sheet, and the four men waiting to lower the coffin looked like the evil characters from the Dickensian novels Leila had read at school.

'Ashes to ashes, dust to dust . . .'

They all stood and waited.

Mary wished that she had known Leila's mother, and Earl screwed up his face in pain at the cold. Then Leila finally closed her eyes and cried. The men rubbed their hands and marched briskly forward to take up their positions at the four corners of the coffin. They lowered it down with little care for the horizontal, and it disappeared into the earth, head first.

The priest beckoned Leila forward. She passed her umbrella to Michael, then took up a damp handful of earth. Again she closed her eyes as she tossed the dirt on to the coffin. It made a sound like rain, only louder. As she opened her eyes and looked down, she saw the other two coffins and her mouth fell open, slowly. Everybody looked at her as she turned and walked the half-dozen paces back towards the priest, with tears of anger now displacing the tears of grief in her eyes. Her voice was unsteady.

'The other coffins,' she pointed. 'What are they doing in my mother's grave?'

'Later,' whispered the priest, his face adopting a sepulchral but understanding smile. He turned over a page of his Bible and adjusted the sheet of plastic.

'Now!' she shouted. 'I want to know now!'

The sheet of plastic gently circled its way into the mud and they both watched it land in complete silence. The only noise was the brittle tap of the rain smacking against the leaves of the trees, and the more resonant plopping as the drops eventually squashed against man-made umbrellas.

The inheritance Leila had expected to receive upon her mother's death was not to be. It turned out her mother had spent what funds she had on bringing them to England. What was left had to be spent on the funeral and the paying of unexpected bills. For Leila the dream of a rich father was a dream buried with her mother. For the first time in her life, Leila found herself troubled about money. Only last week her knowledge of the impending seriousness of the situation had been made apparent.

As usual, Leila and Mary had gone shopping together, not for anything in particular although Mary had talked of buying Calvin some gloves and a scarf. It was when they finally found a stall on the market and they both agreed upon a scarf that Leila discovered she had no money left and Mary, rather than put the scarf back, had insisted upon paying for it.

'No, Mary.'

'Don't be daft. I know you'll give it me back. Anyhow, it's only 1s 6d.'

Leila walked home in silence while Mary jabbered on. Leila had no idea of what she was talking about. They turned into Florence Road and Leila stopped by the door.

'I'll send it round with Val.'

Mary looked at Leila and realized she had worried all this time.

'You know, you're a bundle of nerves. It's not right, Leila. It's really not right at all.'

Inside the house Val stood and offered Calvin to Leila, but for once Leila passed him by unseen. She began to search frantically through the drawers, and on the mantelpiece, and under magazines. Eventually she stopped, feeling on the edge of tears, and she took Calvin from Val but felt too ashamed to tell her about the 1s 6d. So she waited until she heard Val close the front door before slumping down, with Calvin in her arms. She grew darker in herself as the light failed.

That night Michael came home. As he slept Leila stole the 1s 6d from his jacket pocket. She went out into the night, the money in an envelope, and slipped it through Mary's letterbox. Leila came back but she could not sleep, and for two days and two nights she worried herself sick that her deceit would be discovered. But Michael said nothing, and gradually Leila learned to touch Calvin without feeling as if she was dirtying him.

A week later Leila got up and waited until Michael had made his familiar silent exit before she got dressed and turned off the paraffin heater. She took Calvin downstairs and made him something to eat, then she telephoned Mary who hurried around.

'Is it that bad, love? I mean is it definite that you have to go out to work?'

Leila finished changing Calvin.

'I have no money.'

'Well, where does he get his money from, then?'

Leila paused. 'I don't know.'

Mary tutted and shook her head, and Leila took Calvin on her knees and stood him up to block out the look of disbelief she knew Mary was giving her.

'Leila, love, next time you should just tell him that you haven't any money, and you need some or else it'll make you and Calvin poorly. I mean,' said Mary, 'he must be bloody crackers. Does he think you can eat fresh air?'

Leila shrugged her shoulders. She felt humiliated.

Leila signed the papers and saw that her wages would be £11 a week, with overtime a possibility if she wanted it. The man told her that she looked so bony he was putting her on the factory run, to start with, which meant she would ride an empty bus out to the factory to pick up the workmen at the gate. She was to collect the standard fare of 3d and they would drop the workmen off en route back to the depot, and begin again. He gave her the bundle of tickets and told her he usually gave the older women this run. Leila did not know whether she was expected to look grateful or feel insulted.

The bus swung violently off the main road and swept up the gravel drive. It pulled up outside the huge double gates where the men waited impatiently, sheltering from the rain. They jeered ironically as it turned around, then they rushed out like school children and fought among each other, eager to get the best seats. Leila stood back against the luggage-rack as they passed her by on either side. Then she pressed the bell. There were already too many on the bus, but she had lost the control that she had never really had.

As the bus pulled away she decided to take the fares from upstairs first. A barrage of whistles and chanting greeted her as she adjusted her ticket machine.

'Fares, please.'

''Ere, take mine first.'

'No, mine.'

'Fares, please. Any more fares, please?'

'Piss off. Mine's untouched by human hand. Here, love.'

'Any more fares, please? Any more fares?'

Just the short walk up the stairs seemed to have tired Leila, so she turned around and began to walk back down the centre aisle.

'Any more fares? Any more fares, please . . ?'

Her voice cracked and she felt her knees turning to jelly. The cold steel rail burned like ice as she held on tight and lowered herself down the stairs of the bus to the lower floor. Then the jelly melted and she fell and grabbed hold of the pole and clung on for her life as the bus turned a sharp corner. A whistle echoed in her head, and her money flew out of her bag and into the road. Her face seemed only inches away from the tarmac and suddenly she heard the deafening roar of the engine just beside her ears. Two men jumped up, pulled her back on to the bus, and sat her down on the seat they had just left. Upstairs the chanting continued unabated. Downstairs there was silence punctuated only by the solemn shaking of heads and whispered enquiries as to what was the matter with her. Then beads of sweat began to appear on Leila's forehead, even though it was freezing, and then the rain outside turned to hail.

The man looked again at the silver splinter of wood that was a thermometer.

'First day on the job and I would think it might well be your last, Mrs Preston.'

Leila opened her eyes and saw the smooth untroubled outline of his young face, his blue eyes and his tidy, sandy coloured hair that fell away from his forehead. She heard his shoes squeak as he moved away to his desk.

'You can get up now if you like.'

Leila managed to sit up straight. She noticed his teeth, which were chipped, but she had come to expect poor teeth.

'You're not well. You haven't been eating properly.'

The man came towards her and stretched the skin around her eyes.

'No life whatsoever, and you haven't been sleeping, have you?'

Leila looked blankly at him.

'Worst of all, you shouldn't be working if you know that you're going to have a baby.' He smiled conspiratorially at her. Leila lowered her head. His voice sounded like a door closing.

'I'm going to get an ambulance to take you home and I'll have someone call around to see you tomorrow.'

Leila opened her mouth to speak, but the man read her mind and dropped a hand on to her shoulder.

'Now, I didn't say do you want someone to come around and visit you tomorrow. You make sure you're in and not gallavanting off looking for a job on the railways, or the underground, or anything else equally ridiculous.' He moved back to his desk and began to dial. 'The ambulance won't be long.'

Leila closed her eyes and waited. As she did so her tired mind threw itself back to the funeral, and to Earl who had turned up as though it was expected of him, and left as though he had done his duty without ever looking honestly in Leila's direction. It was his eyes that made her despise him, for when he did look they never kept still, as if he were thinking something he was ashamed of. He reminded her of the men, one man in particular, who used to stare at her as she walked through Baytown to get the bus back to St Patrick's.

This was before she took note of Michael, or he of her. The walk back across town to the country bus was made either in solitude or with Millie. Either way the man would stare, but if she were on her own then the stare took on a peculiar ferocity, more a leer, though she did not as yet know the word, and it made her feel she had been attacked, that his hand was already resting in her lap. One day – it was late afternoon – Leila found herself alone and rushing to catch what she imagined would be the last bus to the country. She heard him before she saw him, and he did not really jump, it was more a spring. He flew into her path and stood embarrassed, as if a friend had pushed him there as a practical joke. It was the first time Leila had a close look at him and she realized much to her horror that almost everything about him, from his fingernails to his hair, the corners of his eyes, his clothes, were all dirty, and pity quickly replaced fear in her mind. Somehow she felt happier now that she pitied him, and though he continued to appear occasionally he never again made bold with anything but his eyes.

Leila pitied Earl in the same way. She pitied him but she feared her pity, for if she were to pity every coloured man she saw in England then she would have no space left for any other emotion. It was this that made her dislike him, made her feel weary in his presence, made her look at his sexually hungry eyes. It was only Arthur's eyes, dark and a little mysterious (his own description) that had ever made her feel safe. In them she had seen both innocence and ultimate disappointment which betrayed the well-polished maturity he liked to project. When he first kissed her she felt as though somebody were rubbing sandpaper against her lips. It was her first kiss and in truth she had been satisfied, but it had only raised within her a further curiosity that would need satisfying, though she knew Arthur would never dare do so.

It took nearly a week before he dared to kiss her again, and when he did he tried to make it last longer, like it was a better brand of chewing gum. Leila wanted to giggle as he took her arm. He told her that he thought he loved her; they needed each other, and the island needed them. All Leila could remember was thinking to herself how she had been cheated out of a moment she had read about, a moment which had never been expressed as 'I think I love you' and had never involved anybody else, let alone an island. A week later Arthur tried to touch a breast. As his fingers brushed lightly against

187

her blouse, so lightly that if she objected he could argue it was an accident, Leila threw out her chest, hoping he might take one and give it a small squeeze, or caress it, or do something with it. But he just let his hand touch and pull away, as though he had discovered an as yet uncharted region which would best remain unexplored.

And that was when Leila began to first despise her body, to stand naked in her room as she got dressed in the morning, and as she undressed at night. She would squeeze her own breasts and pretend the hands on the end of her arms were, for five minutes, not her own, the tongue that flicked lazily around her mouth, not her own, the foot that rubbed deliciously up and down the inside of her bare calf, not her own. She grew to hate her body for this assault on itself, feeling that she ought to say something about it to her mother.

Then, when Michael began to stare at her in the street, and the old man who reminded her of Earl gradually began to appear less and less, she stopped touching herself for again she could hope. But Michael took many months before he dared go further than the damp kissing and the touching through clothes after he had taken her back to St Patrick's at night. But when it did happen it was sudden and unexpected, for he appeared as though from nowhere, and demanded that she come with him to Black Rocks on the new bike.

When he woke up Leila reached over to kiss him. He rolled her over on to her back and eased his weight on top of her. She had gasped with pain. His body was heavy and still leaden with sleep. She could feel him rubbing himself against her, his trousers bulging with something that felt to her like a live tree stump. But she did not touch it, or want to touch it, for it felt large and unpredictable. As Michael coaxed her pants down to her ankles, and as she heard him unbuttoning his trousers, Leila closed her eyes tight and prayed it would be like in the books. If it was she would be able to face her mother with a knowledge that she had gleaned before. Her familiarity would withstand any line of questioning and offset any future staring from old men.

But now Michael no longer bothered to force himself upon her. It was as if she were a tunnel he was tired of passing through. Leila's fears as to why this might be had recently been proved true.

Somehow she had always expected to smell a cheap scent, or find a letter, or notice a smear of lipstick on Michael's face, but it was a hair that she had found, a light hair curled delicately, a nest almost in itself, on the shoulder of his jacket. She must have rested her head next to his, cheek to cheek, and maybe they danced. Maybe it had been cold and he had given her the jacket to wear and keep herself warm as he walked her home one night, but Leila did not know. All she knew was the woman, or one of the women, was blonde, or had made herself blonde with hair dye.

Although she had her ideas of what the woman probably looked like, although she wanted to meet her (though what she would say she had no idea), it was not this blonde woman who had occupied her thoughts as she carefully lifted the hair. It was Mary, nearly fifty, her hair greying in streaks rather than flecks, her bare legs nearly always sticking out from beneath an old skirt. She wondered, albeit for a second, if Mary thought the same things about Michael that the blonde woman did. What would happen if Mary were twenty years younger, or Michael twenty years older? Would Mary take the jacket and slip it around her shoulders as she walked along the Embankment by the Thames? Leila was, without even realizing it, making an enemy in her mind of the only real friend she had in England.

And then she thought of Val who was suddenly both more and less of a threat, her age and assumed inexperience signalling innocence, her maturity to come, danger.

As far as Leila could remember Mary had never said anything to her about any men, white or coloured, other than

Michael and Harry. It was as though she was not interested in them, having long since outgrown seeing them as either something to be attracted to or repulsed from. Leila had always found this a relief, especially as she had been led to believe that all white women in England loved coloured men. Millie had once said to her, 'It was like playing with tiger instead of dog but I bet you a few of them going get bitten.'

Leila had laughed then, but, as the ambulance came and her first and last day at work on the buses ended, she found precious little to laugh about. When the ambulance arrived at Florence Road Leila felt no better.

Mary rushed out to meet her, but Leila looked blankly at her. She walked into the house and sat down. Mary held her hand. Leila trembled and her mind drifted, cloud-like. Mary left her in the front room and went to put the kettle on. As they waited for the water to boil Leila bit her lower lip and tried not to look up. She felt pathetic.

The next day Leila sat on the settee in her dressing gown and drank a cup of coffee with Miss Gordon, the social worker whom the doctor had sent to visit her. Miss Gordon looked to Leila to be in her mid-forties. She dressed from shoulder to calf in wool and tweed. On top she gathered her hair into an unhealthily tidy bun, and she hid most of her freckled face behind a pair of black horn-rimmed spectacles. As she waited for Leila to answer her questions she kept crossing and uncrossing her legs. She sighed, then once again her sharp Scottish accent droned forth and Leila felt as though she was listening to a musical instrument being played out of tune.

'So, Mrs Preston, everything with yourself and Calvin is alright today, then? I mean, there's nothing I could get done for you in the way of a bit of shopping, is there?'

Leila shook her head as if keen to give up talking for good. Miss Gordon tried again.

'Have you seen your husband lately, Mrs Preston?' Her

client was not responding, so Miss Gordon tried to make it easier. 'Has he been around to give you any money lately? Yesterday, for instance?' Leila smiled. 'Has he got a job, Mrs Preston?' Miss Gordon scraped stocking against stocking.

'Has he been around here to give you money for Calvin and yourself, and for the extra food that you'll be having to eat if you're to look after the child in your tummy?' Leila put down her coffee cup. Miss Gordon sighed.

'You haven't told him, have you?'

Leila looked down at the floor like a schoolgirl being chastised for turning up at games without her gym kit.

'I haven't seen him.'

'At all?' asked Miss Gordon, feeling that at last she was making some progress. Leila felt this too, so she shut up. Miss Gordon changed the subject.

'Would you like to come for a walk with me to put some flowers on your mother's grave?'

Leila looked up at her as if Miss Gordon had just asked her the time, then she began to laugh and Miss Gordon knew that she ought to leave now. She stood up and began to fasten her coat.

'Well, thank you for the coffee, dear, and I'll be seeing you again on Monday. If Mr Preston does call around, could you tell him that I'd like to have him ring me? You have the number, but if he isn't able to take it for any reason, then could you please try and keep him here until I arrive? I'll leave my card on the side just in case.'

Miss Gordon took out a slim volume of cards from her purse and placed one by the telephone. Then she adjusted her collar and turned to the resting Calvin.

'Now you be a good boy for your mummy, Calvin, and don't you be waking up in the middle of the night and disturbing her.' Miss Gordon looked at Leila. 'I'll be off now.'

Leila glanced away and said nothing. She listened for the

door closing. Then she heard Miss Gordon's shoes click against the sidewalk as she passed by the window.

The thought of being pregnant again filled Leila with something, though it was neither fear nor happiness. Resignation was the word she had come most often to use, for any question of disposing of the child was, of course, out of the question. Back home Leila had heard of women who did such things, and of women who did it to them, but these people were few and far between, not a regular part of the day-to-day circular life of the island. Her resignation caused her to think about Calvin and her long pregnancy with him, nine months which seemed to her about equal in length to the rest of her life put together, for her mind had been occupied not only with the child her body held, but also with the child of another woman.

Beverley's child was a boy; nobody had actually told her this, but Leila knew, and she constantly wondered how it was he had been conceived. She was sure that Michael must have come to Beverley late at night, not because he was being secretive, simply because this would have been more romantic, and perhaps they had even talked first. Then Beverley, wearing only a light dress, would have come over and sat in his lap and he would have twisted around the ends of her spiky hair with his fingers until they curled and sprang of their own accord. Maybe this annoyed her a little, but she said nothing. Then, without turning down the gas lamp or blowing out the candles (Leila had never been in Beverley's house), they would have eased across the room and into the bedroom, leaving the door open so they could still see each other. They would have stripped off their clothes and lain together just touching, as if giving each other small electric shocks. This was how Leila imagined Beverley's child to have been conceived; but the most disturbing thing was she still managed to think of herself, at some time distant and unknown, with a man (she no longer entertained the possibility that it might be Michael), going through the same ritual. But she could not for the life of her imagine either when, or where, or how.

Beverley must have looked at her child, Leila thought, and felt happy to see Michael's features in him rather than try desperately to pretend that they were not there. She must have looked into his eyes and seen his father's eyes rather than search for her own reflection; and when Beverley held her child she probably held him with her fingertips so that he was ready to be shared when the time came. Then, as her body shrivelled back to its former size, Beverley must have smiled, Leila thought, she must have smiled and shared a laugh with nature, knowing that her body would soon be full again.

And now, in England, Leila climbed from her bed each morning and looked down at her body, which seemed to her like a dull balloon someone was slowly blowing life into. It would, over the months, expand and take its shape, and though she might feel as if she were going to burst, she knew nature would relieve the pressure at just the right moment. She knew also that Michael would not be with her when this happened, but she could not be sure of who exactly it would be. Perhaps Mary, perhaps Millie again, perhaps nobody. The one thing about which Leila could, among all of this, be sure was that her pregnancy was real. She felt the pain, and the aches, and the slowness, and she knew there was little for her to do but accept it: and this she knew she would do for, like the rest of her life, much of it revolved around this resignation and this waiting.

It was early afternoon now, and Miss Gordon was forgotten. Leila panicked, suddenly afraid the woman might have taken Calvin. He was asleep by her side. Not only was he her son, he was also her best friend, and soon they would be three. Leila left him and went up to the bathroom. She bent over the sink and ran out some cold water into her cupped hands and splashed it on to her face. Then she took up her seat on the toilet bowl and again she tried to think of a time when she could imagine herself being happy in England with two children, and no father, and little money. Again she tried to imagine what it would be like if Michael put his hand on her shoulder, and said, 'Sorry,' and explained to her why he behaved as he did. Again she tried to imagine how she could live back home without her mother, but eventually she would always try and remind herself that she had retired from such sport, that an empty mind was the safest mind, continued speculation futile. She closed her eyes.

Perhaps, thought Leila, she just wanted to walk across Michael's body like an English county she had never explored. Leila tried hard to picture what she looked like, sure in her mind that she would resemble the women at the bus stops, swathed in winter coats which hid bodies so shapeless it looked to her as though they concealed sacks of potatoes. And she was sure she would be like the other English women she had seen who always seemed to comb their hair when coloured men were around, or smile their crooked smiles, their lips like dried wood, as if they were trying to attract something. Leila did not understand these women, except as a threat to her, but what it was they were threatening she was not sure, for she had only one man, and she had barely held on to him even back home where the likelihood of a white woman taking her husband was remote and beyond consideration. But when she thought like this Leila knew she was lying to herself, for the thing that stopped her looking in the mirror on a morning was what was being threatened by these potato women. That was herself, and what she was. If it had been simply a question of Michael, then these women would have left her mind less troubled.

Leila had noticed that a white person's face holds thin and visibly broken red veins, split and tired, scratched all over it like a map with only the smallest rivers marked upon it; it sports cracked thin lips drained of blood, and from the legs sprout small feet, even if the toes are big. In England Leila had suddenly found herself, her light skin starved of the sun, growing paler by the day. But she was more coloured than she had ever been before, and not shame exactly, but feelings of inadequacy prevented her from looking back into the mirror. These feelings were not entirely new for she had occasionally hidden behind a tree and watched the white women on the beaches toasting their skins in the sun, coating their bodies in the sweet-smelling oil and waiting until the sun made them coloured like her. But it was not until she reached her teens that she began to come to terms with the illogical desire behind their behaviour (but this was not until she had actually tried the lying down in the sun with the oil for herself). It was funny, though, but she could never remember any of the white men being brown. They tried, but at the end of the day their stubbornly white bodies peeled themselves clear of the beach, moist sand clinging to the backs of their legs and arms, their faces still drooping with flabby white skin. Like albino walruses they would follow their wives back to their hotel, burdened down with towels and unread books. Leila had looked upon these white people as if they were an endangered species. She spied on them, but here in England she saw them all the time, yet she still did not understand them any better than she did when she was a young girl. She did not understand them any better than she did her husband.

Once, when Leila had wandered off after school on her own, she had spoken to an old white lady down by the quayside. She had noticed her glasses for they were round and made of wire, and to Leila they looked like gold so she came closer. The lady was dressed in a thick blue skirt with a blouse to match. On top of her head she wore an elaborate and gaudily decorated hat. At first she did not see the small girl who was edging her way around her, but when she did she smiled and held out her empty hand as if offering the child a sweet. Leila scurried forward but tried not to look cheated when she saw there was nothing in the lady's hand.

'What's your name?'

Leila scratched a hard line in the dust with the outside of her sandal.

'Sally? Is that your name? Or Gertrude?'

Leila began to giggle and she let her head fall to one side so she could look up at the lady better.

'Don't be scared of me? Are you scared of me?'

'No,' said Leila, her high voice sharp and confident.

'Good, you're a good little girl, aren't you?'

Leila laughed, her eyes all the time fixed upon the lady. 'Are you a witch?' she asked in that trilling accusative voice that only a child has the ability to muster. 'Are you a witch?'

This time she shouted but the lady tried hard not to panic, her smile long since firmly sewn to her lips. Leila laughed again and skipped away to find the school bus, knowing she would not tell any of her friends of her adventure. It would remain a secret.

That night her mother woke suddenly and heard Leila screaming. She dashed quickly from her room to Leila's bedside. She cradled her only daughter in her arms, rocking her back and forth, whispering for her to calm down. But when Leila finally settled again, and her mother asked her what was the matter, Leila said nothing. She would not tell in case she was smacked for behaving badly, and the conversation they should have had then was, like so many others, postponed until it was now too late.

*

Leila got up, made Calvin his breakfast, waited for the postman to bring nothing, thought of Michael, read a page or two of a book, walked in the cold to her mother's grave, came back, made Calvin something else to eat, then sat in the gloom waiting for it to get dark before going to bed. This was her life.

Occasionally Miss Gordon would call but often she would pretend not to be in. When Miss Gordon did catch her in, the conversation was always the same predictable game of 'Have you seen your husband, Mrs Preston?', 'Is Calvin alright, Mrs Preston?', 'You're only twenty, Mrs Preston', 'Do you have any money, Mrs Preston?', 'You know I do so adore coloured babies, Mrs Preston'. Leila would look at her, knowing that soon Miss Gordon might be wearing a uniform and waiting for trains to arrive at Victoria Station, that is, if coloured people were still coming to this country. She would feel as though she had something to offer. Perhaps she did, thought Leila, but not to her.

Leila's only other visitor was Mary. But after the funeral it seemed to Leila that her once closest friend had begun to keep her distance and the differences between them were becoming more obvious. Leila would steal a look at Mary as she passed by the window on her way to the shops. She seemed to be getting older with every journey, looking her age, and then tragically, on one journey, looking older than her age.

Leila's mind followed her, and eventually Mary turned the corner and as she did so Leila's mind turned a corner and she left behind many things. Michael, a man whose feelings for her had been like a knife at her throat for over two years now. He failed not only to see her but to speak to her. His mind, though obviously burdened, was something she was now denied access to. She imagined that day-to-day life was probably as frustrating for him as it was for her, and though she could forgive him for taking temporary refuge in the arms of another woman, and though she could forgive him his drunkenness and abusiveness, she could not forgive him all of these things at once, and she could never hope to understand them if he could not see her, or talk to her even. Her marriage was dead, though it had probably only managed to breathe at all by drawing upon the artificial cylinder of blind hope. His footsteps became more distant, the echoing of his shoes lighter, missing first one beat and then another, until they finally faded altogether.

Then Leila left England behind, not understanding this country in which a smile could mean six things at once, a nudge on a bus from a stranger either an accident or a prologue to a series of events that might actually lead to your destruction. In England people left bread on their doorsteps and dogs came and passed water on it, and in England it never rained good and hard. Leila could no longer stand and watch the drips fall from her forehead and down into her eyes.

Mary posed to Leila the hardest part of her new life to consider, for now more than ever before she was white, and Michael's woman was white (the hair blonde). Even without knowing it Mary might hurt her in some way, for she had come too close to Leila, and Leila cursed herself for being foolish enough to allow this to happen. Mary's voice alone, not even her presence, would always worry her, and what now followed would be in Leila's mind as strained and as artificial as their first meetings were honest and spontaneous. Leila thought again of the uniformed women at the train station, then Mary, and then Mary's continual help and generosity, then the women at the station, then Mary again, all in quick succession, trying to root her among cruel and stupid people, but Mary would not stay still. The moments of help and the laughter they had shared came flooding back.

Then she imagined Michael's woman, then a young Mary, and she tried to make the two of them mix into one, but Mary was not blonde, and Leila's unconscious desire to unravel her friend from such a fate held true. Then she saw Mary pretending to be asleep on the beach, the man talking to Leila, and Leila's mother about to appear standing over them, and this seemed to fit better, but it was the thought of Miss Gordon that finally enabled Leila to drown her friend Mary.

198

mixing - cultures etc.

Miss Gordon could never pretend to be anything other than what she was; a missionary whom Leila had read about in books when she did history back home. Often, when Leila had refused to answer the door, Miss Gordon could be heard knocking on Mary's door and it would be a long while, often half an hour before Miss Gordon's distinctive feet could be heard clip-clopping out of Mary's house and past Leila's window. Betrayal, thought Leila, was perhaps too strong a word to use, but Leila felt cheated by Mary's clandestine meetings. Because Mary talked with Miss Gordon she could be made to fit Michael's woman, the woman on the beach, the uniformed women, and she could lie with Miss Gordon in Leila's mind.

And Miss Gordon herself; Leila dare not touch her, sure that she would sting her with her bitter concern. Full of good will, she infected Leila and Calvin with it, and when she touched Calvin (which she loved to do) Leila was sure that it was done to see if his skin colour was invented or real, to see if his blood was cold, for as she touched him she always let her hand slide a little as if scraping up a laboratory sample underneath her fingernails. When she talked to Leila in that high Scots voice, she always swallowed either just before or just after the word coloured, as if ashamed of it, and Leila felt sure that when she spoke to her parents about her work she steeled her face when she reached the word coloured, and when she wrote it down she put it in inverted commas. After a glass of wine with her friends, if she had any friends, she probably giggled at the word, but with Leila it always got caught just beneath the centre of her tongue and created more saliva than the rest of the words in the sentence put together. As she had talked more than once with Mary, Leila wondered if Miss Gordon had used the word with her. If she had asked her how she felt about living next to coloured people, and if Mary had offered to make her a cup of tea.

On this morning a cold wind burrowed down the road, tearing bits of paper out of the gutter and whirling them around like winter kites. Miss Gordon did not call, and Leila made Calvin his breakfast, then tried to encourage him to sleep. She sat patiently with him until his restlessness died down and he closed his eyes. She could tell it was cold outside. She had heard it rain. She felt Calvin's unease was a result of the weather. Leila shivered, the chill running both ways along the length of her spine but settling nowhere. Then she went across to the fireplace where there was enough wood and coal to light just one more fire.

Leila swept the grate clean and began to twist up pieces of newspaper and lay them down as a base. The bits of wood she arranged neatly and tent-like on top of the paper. Then she took a match to the architecture and watched the whole thing begin to flare up. Holding open a double sheet of newspaper in front of the grate she created a vacuum, and the fire began to rise. She heard the wood snap in pain. Leila decided to clear out the upstairs first.

She stripped the pillowcases off from the pillows and held one open. Then she took it across to the wardrobe and filled it with all the clothes that she had bought for herself since coming to England. There was not much, just a scarf, a pair of gloves and a jumper. She took out Michael's clothes from the wardrobe, then she emptied her drawer of unanswered and half-written letters. The drawer beneath hers was full of Calvin's English clothes, and she stuffed what she could in the pillowcase until it was full. The room did not look all that different; the furniture was still there, as were the pictures of her mother, but it felt cleaner.

Leila shut the door and she carried the pillowcase downstairs. She began to feed the fire with the objects and garments that reminded her of her five months in England. The room became warm and Leila began to laugh as she searched everywhere finding new things to drop in the now empty pillowcase. A bunch of plastic flowers, a shopping bag, a small vase, a set of ashtrays; and in the kitchen cups, food, anything. Things that would not burn like cutlery, pots and pans she left, for she did not need to get rid of everything. What would not fit into her suitcase she would simply abandon. And what she would abandon she would not need. As she watched objects flare, then finally die, blacken, then flake, Leila fell asleep, sure that she could hear the sound of the sea. But it was a dull repetitive knocking that woke her, and she moved sluggishly to the door.

'Can I come in?'

Leila stepped back to let her pass. She shut the door behind her. Mary smiled anxiously as she wandered into the front room, but she had to control herself for it no longer looked like a home, more like a cheap hotel room. She sat heavily on the settee and looked at Calvin who was asleep in his cot. It seemed as though Leila lived in this one room now, for the settee was partially made up like a bed and Leila's things were strewn all over. Calvin's toys and his dirty washing were lying in a heap in the middle of the floor, and there was no heating apart from the signs of a now dying fire in the grate. Gradually Mary forced herself to look across at Leila whose skin, once a milky coffee colour, now looked pale. Leila looked back at her and let a smile break out on her face which seemed to say, 'So what?' Mary looked away. For her the day drifted by unused, wasted in silence. Leila, on the other hand, felt alert, convinced that if she turned around quickly enough she would see her mother.

That night the wind howled. Neither mother nor son slept. They merely waited for the darkness to lift. When it did Leila dressed her son warmly in what clothes remained. She could feel the cold inside the house and she knew it would be even colder outside. Having dressed him, she laid him down on the dry half of the settee (for by now she had grown accustomed to waking up with her thighs smelling

201

and her body damp with urine). Calvin was too cold to smell his mother. He played by himself and waited anxiously for her attention as she pulled on her thin jacket. She came to him and they locked the door behind them. They began their familiar walk through the streets that Leila imagined her husband and his blonde woman so happily wandered when nobody else was around.

People in the streets were busy, hurrying everywhere. They all rushed, for it was Christmas. The cars slushed past throwing up a spray of melted ice and water, leaving their tracks seemingly indelibly etched into the road. Then another car would come along and scratch the same message, then another, till they became like the people, one huge pattern of individual marks, each indistinguishable from the next, each reduced with the short passing of time from being a proud something to being a distant untraceable blur.

Leila stopped at a window and listened to her son speaking, though he could not as yet speak. She watched his image reflected in the glass as he spoke with unsurity.

'Mommy, is that Santa Claus there, that man with the white beard and moustache, that man with a red suit and a red face?'

She held Calvin so he would be able to see better. His short arm freed itself from being trapped between his own small body and his mother's breasts. It pointed out the man he was talking about.

'Him, mommy, that man there with the funny horse.'

Leila looked at her son, his eyes bright, his face eager for knowledge.

'Yes, Calvin, that's Santa Claus,' said Leila.

Calvin looked at her as she confirmed the man's identity, then he looked back at the man.

'Why is Santa Claus white?'

Leila could not answer her own question.

'He should be coloured. Why isn't Santa Claus coloured?'

Leila began to repeat herself like a record player stuck into a groove. She tore other parents' and other children's attention away from the man. They just looked at her and moved away, saying nothing.

'Why isn't Santa Claus coloured?' she whispered.

She walked heavily up the long hill, then through the tall iron gates. Gothic trees, their roots muscular and visible, lined the drive. The cemetery was empty.

The stiff wind folded the short grass and the arms of the trees shivered. Leila's breath clouded and rose, and she stood, Calvin in her arms, underneath the now familiar oak tree. She crept towards her mother's grave and knelt. Leila had no flowers. She never brought any, fearful that someone might mistake them as belonging to one of the other occupants, but she had her memories. Underneath where it said the names of the two other people she read her mother's own name and cried. Her mother was more than mere scratchings on soft English stone.

One day Leila knew she would meet her again and be able to tell her that. If they could not be equals as mothers then maybe they might find equality of some kind in their death. But first Leila would take a boat and leave Michael in this country among the people who seemed to keep him warm in mind and body. England, in whom she had placed so much of her hope, no longer held for her the attraction of her mother and new challenges. At least the small island she had left behind had safety and two friends, and if the price to be paid for this was a stern predictability from one day to the next then she was ready to pay it.

The child in her body and the one in her arms would never know of Michael. But she was sure that nobody would blame her for this. When the time did come when her children would ask her questions she could not answer, she would take them down to the harbour and wait with them, as the ship lay offshore, waiting. She would watch as they climbed into the small boat and made their way out to the ship and on to England to find a Michael, or men like him who might give them the answers they sought. She would continue to wait for them, holding Millie's hand, both their hair grey and hidden (Bradeth also grey, at home, waiting for Millie), knowing that being her boys (she had never entertained the possibility of a daughter) they would come back to her with the next tide. Then together, the three of them (mother, son, son) would make their way back to St Patrick's and sit and wait for night to fall, having finally, at the end of her day, shared something that she knew was beyond her or anyone else's explanation. Leila looked again at her mother's simple tombstone and from it she drew the extra strength that enabled her to get to her feet.

Leila left the cemetery the same way that she had come in, through the tall iron gates. On her way home she did not stop to listen to the carols or to buy presents. She walked quickly through the back streets, wanting to keep off the main roads and away from people. Calvin was asleep in her arms and the baby she carried in her body felt heavy.

The bitter December air bruised Leila's face. She stopped. It was beginning to get dark, and the streetlights had not yet been switched on. The only illumination was provided by the Christmas trees which lit up the windows of the houses in Florence Road. From around the corner a lorry sped into view and hurtled past them. They must have looked strangely eerie in the winter's dusk, standing there unmoving, woman, child, child to be. Then the snowflakes began to spin, first one, then tens of them. Leila watched spellbound. Then she fled into the house and locked the door behind her.

A speckled, burnished light crept in off the street, piercing the awful inadequacy of the curtains. Leila caught sight of herself in a mirror. She looked like a yellowing snapshot of an old relative, fading with the years. She turned suddenly and saw that somebody had pushed a Christmas card through the front door. She stooped, with Calvin, and picked it up and read it, but it was from nobody.